Stuart worked for forty years in further and higher education, first as a lecturer, progressing to becoming a university principal lecturer and eventually a university pro vice chancellor (vice president), before retiring from full-time work in 2010. Stuart is widely published in the academic world, but *A Shoelace, a Paper Clip and a Pencil* is his first foray into fiction. For his 'sins', as he says, he supports his hometown soccer team West Bromwich Albion and (sometimes) enjoys playing golf. He lives between York in Northern England and their house in Spain with his wife Dilys.

TO MY BEAUTIFUL WIFE, DILYS

Stuart C. Billingham

A SHOELACE, A PAPER CLIP AND A PENCIL

AUSTIN MACAULEY PUBLISHERS™

LONDON • CAMBRIDGE • NEW YORK • SHARJAH

A CIP catalogue record for this title is available from the British Library.

ISBN 9781528981040 (Paperback)
ISBN 9781528981057 (ePub e-book)

www.austinmacauley.com

First Published (2020)
Austin Macauley Publishers Ltd
25 Canada Square
Canary Wharf
London
E14 5LQ

Friends and family have read and commented on drafts of various parts of the early manuscript. Without their help, it would not be the work it is, but any flaws or weaknesses are entirely my responsibility.

My sister, Carole Buckingham, my two very good friends, Hilary Frayling and Sue Thompson, and my old friend, John Dickens. Many thanks to you all.

Many friends were also interested in what I was doing, and I do thank you all for the encouragement that gave me along the way.

And, of course, I must thank those people who have found themselves in the book, albeit with different names. I am sure you will recognise yourselves in the pages that follow.

But my most important supporter has been my wife, Dilys, to whom this book is humbly dedicated.

Dilys was not just my main proof-reader but also did much of the research to ensure aspects of the work are as accurate as they can be. I can imagine she dreaded the now famous call from our study, "Dilys. Are you busy?" She always allowed me plenty of time and space to do the writing and thinking. Most important of all, she was the one who encouraged me to write the story in the first place. Without her, there wouldn't be *A Shoelace, a Paper Clip and a Pencil*. Thank you my darling.

Part One

Chapter One
February 2002

Tom and Jane were walking back to the railway station after a very successful meeting with other senior managers from the region's universities, and were deep in conversation about the next stages. It was potentially exciting stuff. They came to a large junction and waited for the lights to turn in their favour. It was unusually quiet in the city—the aftermath of the Christmas and New Year holidays taking their toll on everyone's spending—and with unusually very little traffic.

The pedestrian walking-light turned green and off they set. Five or six seconds later, a car screeched around the corner. It hit Jane—a glancing blow, knocking her backwards and sideways, towards the pavement she had just left. It hit Tom full-on, as he had turned to see what the hell was happening. He was thrown into the air and across the bonnet—a gruesome replay of all those stunts he had seen in the movies. He landed on the road very near to Jane, as the car continued its journey, more-or-less without a pause. All that could now be seen were two crumpled piles of humanity, with limbs lying in peculiar and seemingly impossible positions, and blood seeping slowly from beneath them.

Within moments, there were blue lights and sirens blaring all around them—though neither of them heard or saw any of it.

Chapter Two
July 2001

"It should be left, over a bridge, at the end of this street," said Liz.

Tom stopped the car outside the bottle-green, wide, wooden door, about halfway down a narrow, partly-cobbled street, pretty much as described in the holiday brochure. He rang the large bell-pull hanging to the left of the magnificent old door, which created an echoing sound from inside the building, reminiscent of those in the old black-and-white horror movies he had seen on TV.

After a nervous 'is anyone there' moment, they heard footsteps from within. The door was opened very slowly, by a slender, well-dressed, grey-haired woman, probably in her late 50s.

"Ah, Mr Cooper I presume," a phrase he couldn't help associating with that famous exploration in Africa. "Please, do come this way. Do you have luggage from the car?"

"Not much. Just a case and an overnight bag which we have here with us on the pavement."

"Fine. Please, bring the bags inside. Daan will show you where to park your car later."

They followed the silver-haired lady across a large, partly wood-panelled hall, with a marvellous dark-blue, grey and cream ceramic, tiled floor, to a small door at its far end.

Of what they could see so far, the house was magnificent in that faded-glory way of many older French properties. It also had a smell which Tom always associated with being in old French houses—a mixture of old wood and damp, with a background hint of garlic and olive oil and freshly baked bread. Tom had no idea how those smells could combine in every old French house he'd been in, but they certainly did. The house was pretty dark with several shuttered windows, so they made their way carefully, following the grey-haired woman up the narrow stone stairs which led from the small hallway door. After climbing four flights, they emerged into 'La Tour'.

'La Tour' was the castellated tower, with the classical steep, conical shape and tiled roof, situated at the western end of the house and protruding well above it. It was let to holidaymakers in the French 'Gites' tradition—a self-contained apartment but, in this case, with the security of the owners living in the same property to help with any problems. As Tom knew from past experience, old buildings could produce unexpected problems, even for the wary. Having someone on hand to help with any such things was partly what had attracted them to this place. This holiday was about relaxing—not running around doing emergency 'DIY' repairs.

"I'll let you have a look around for a while to see if you like our little gem. I'll be back in ten minutes or so, if that's OK?" said the lady.

"Thank you. Fine with us," said Liz.

They now stood facing a huge room with arched and leaded casement windows with massive stone windowsills—easily deep enough to sit on—and a very high, half-timbered ceiling. The walls were painted beige and it was furnished comfortably and in very good taste. There was a good-sized, old, oak table at one end of the room near to the kitchen area which was partly separated from the main room by a small breakfast bar. At the other end was a really sumptuous-looking, three-seater settee and an equally comfortable-looking armchair—both with 'throws' and cushions, in an intriguingly patterned cotton or maybe linen material. There was also a small coffee table and a couple of tall, wide and fairly-full bookshelves. Tom thought the dark, oak, wooden floor looked like the original 18th century when the chateau had been built—or so the brochure had said. He glanced at Liz who smiled contentedly. It was clear that this had been a good choice.

Tom and Liz had been married for only a handful of years. For both, Tom in his late-40s, Liz in her mid-50s, this was second time around. They met on a trip to the States, organised by the university in which they both worked as lecturers to try and identify possible new university partnerships over there.

It certainly hadn't been love at first sight, and after they returned to the UK, Tom had quite a job in the courting stakes. First, because they lived about 60 or so miles from each other—Tom commuted that distance to work at the main campus whilst Liz lived just a local bus ride from it. And second, because Liz clearly believed he needed a much younger partner—and tried hard to find him one! Eventually though, and as some Americans in Georgia where they first met might say, "He got his gal." They got married pretty soon after that and then, only a couple of years later, came a move from their university so that Tom could take up a new senior position at another one, some 90 miles south. After they had moved, Liz went into part-time teaching at a local college on the edge of the city.

The last two years since the move had been frantically busy, and this holiday was meant to allow them to chill-out properly—really for the first time in that time. The trip through France had been smooth and uneventful—"Well, if you discount the flat tyre on the outskirts of Clermont Ferrand that is," as Tom was prone to say to anyone who asked. Now came ten days of resting in the shadow of the Pyrenees. Time to recuperate, eat well, drink good wine and simply 'be', before meandering back home via several stops, staying in pre-booked hotels in beautiful parts of France.

"It's wonderful," said Liz, "Really wonderful. Just what we had hoped for and more."

"Thank you," said the grey-haired lady, who had returned as promised, though not, as Liz noted, before knocking at their door. *A nice touch,* she thought.

"You are not the first to say so, but thank you so much. It means a lot. Unless you are too tired from your journey, maybe you would join Daan and I for aperitifs in our Conservatory. Shall we say, in an hour or so, around six?"

"Thank you," said Tom, "That is very kind, er… Madame Eyck."

"My first name is Boukje. Pronounced *bough-ki-ye*, or at least, that will be near enough," she laughed.

"And I am Tom, and this is Liz."

"I'll come and get you about 6 pm then."

Chapter Three

"Welcome. Do come in," said a mild but unmistakably male voice. Tom, Liz and Boukje entered a very large conservatory.

Wine, olives and canapés were laid out on a small table which was surrounded by baroque-style chairs. The room was light and airy, comfortably warm and inviting. Many pot plants, including some very large ferns alongside much smaller plants—mainly green rather than with flowers—were arranged around three sides of the room. It felt exactly as intended, as if you were sitting partly in, and partly looking into a garden. On the other house sidewall stood a very large and beautifully carved oak sideboard, which would have graced any large, well-appointed dining room, furnished in the right genre. It was adorned with a couple of bottles of wine, plus some lovely decanters—probably of whiskey, brandy, or rum—all chaperoned by different types of expensive-looking cut glasses.

Through the glass walls and past the indoor plants, it was possible to see the gardens of the house. They were not especially large, but composed of a mixture of hard landscaping and various shrubs and trees. It was all slightly dishevelled. *A bit like Daan,* Tom thought, as he moved towards Daan's outstretched hand.

Everyone shook hands, with Tom giving Boukje a peck on both cheeks and Daan doing the same with Liz—the usual formal greeting between men and women in continental Europe.

"Do take a seat," said Daan, pointing at the chairs around the small table. "And what would you like to drink?" Boukje had a gin and tonic, Liz asked for a small white wine, Tom asked for a red wine and Daan had a gin and tonic too. Before long, they were all settled around the canapes and nibbles, and chatting like friends who hadn't seen each other for a while.

Conversation was easy and flowed naturally, starting as is always the case in such situations, with tales of Tom and Liz's journey and then polite questions about each other. As the G&Ts and wine—and Daan's topping up of glasses—began to take effect, the conversation became even more relaxed and familiar. Daan and Boukje heard of Tom and Liz's whirlwind romance; Tom briefly described his working past—with the Home Office and various educational institutions, and Liz shared her journey from being a single mum rearing two young boys, to becoming a senior lecturer at the university.

Daan and Boukje's spoken English was impeccable, but still, with that hint of a northern European language lurking in the background. They had lived and worked for several years in the US. Daan had been the international correspondent for a national broadsheet in the Netherlands and Boukje had worked in a senior management position for a travel company. Daan had then been offered and accepted a European correspondent position with the *New York Times*. Boukje knew that she could find work in the travel industry almost anywhere in the world and perhaps, especially in the States. She had many connections. So, they had moved there.

"Upped sticks and went," said Daan, "That's what you would say, isn't it?" Tom and Liz laughed and said, "Absolutely!" They all laughed together.

Daan shared exciting tales of his role, both with the paper in the Netherlands and with the NYT. He regaled them with his conversations with members of the Mafia in Sicily and Milan, of interviews with famous politicians such as Willy Brandt and even being chased through the streets of Paris by an international gang of smugglers after he had exposed their various activities across Europe. He also revealed, with a wry and sardonic grin aimed at Tom and Liz, the 'exceptionally exciting times' he had reporting on the work of the European Commission and the European Parliament.

Boukje, not wanting to be left out, told stories of various hotels in which she had worked for the travel company before being elevated to her management post, of a plague of rats and other vermin in the kitchens and stores of one of the largest and oldest (and easily most expensive) hotels in Egypt, blithely ignored by its management until a tourist saw them and blew the whistle, of suspected terrorists masquerading as normal holidaymakers in a beachside hotel in Gran Canaria and of the sexual exploits of the 18-25 club in various stages of undress, revealing various (normally clothed) parts of their bodies, in various postures and in various public places in Ibiza. Tom and Liz had been around, but this story left them wide-eyed and gaping like two goldfish.

After an hour or so of 'the adventures of Boukje and Daan', Boukje asked if they would like to see around the house—at least, those parts which were not let.

For both Liz and Tom, it was, quite simply, unbelievable. Each room was a treasure-trove of antique furniture; beautiful and unusual fabrics drawn from different periods, styles and different cultures, collected over many years of travel and rummaging at markets. The culturally diverse fabrics, furniture and other things in each room sat not only comfortably, but splendidly side by side. The structure of each room had been lovingly restored to be as close as possible to what it would have been in the 18th or early 19th century. The fireplaces, for example, were remarkable given the state of disrepair; they were in when Boukje and Daan first saw them—revealed to Tom in some photos Daan shared with him. Tom had done some similar work at his house in Halton, just outside Lancaster, and knew just what a lot of work it was. Tom thought that 'lovingly' would be a good way to describe how the house had been restored.

"It is remarkable. Really magnificent," said Tom and Liz almost simultaneously.

"Thank you," said Daan, "It is always a great pleasure to invite guests like you into our home—people who appreciate what we have tried to do here."

During the tour of their home, Tom, Liz, Boukje and Daan had not only chatted about the house and all its glories, but had continued to discuss various parts of their lives.

Unsurprisingly, perhaps Daan was especially astute at seeking out a story, and both Tom and Liz had several to share. At this stage, nothing quite as dramatic as the 18-25 club or being chased through Paris by mobsters, it had to be said.

After the house tour, the four of them wended their way back to 'La Tour'. Once there, Daan opened the door and gave a short but meaningful glance towards Boukje.

"You guys look tired to me and I am not surprised," he said. "Time for you to settle into what will be your new home for the next few days. We will not, how do you say, 'bother you' from now on… Unless you need us, and then you can call us on the phone just here." He pointed to the intercom on the wall, "Or on our mobiles, the numbers you have, I think."

"Thank you, Daan. And for such a wonderful evening. Yes, 'time for bed', as a famous cartoon character for kids in the UK used to say. But Liz and I would very much like to return the compliment of your hospitality this evening," said Tom. Daan and Boukje looked quizzically at him. "Perhaps you would join us one evening in 'La Tour' for wine and nibbles?"

"Ah," said Daan, "that would be very good, eh Boukje?"

"Very pleased to do that," said Boukje.

"I have a story," said Tom, "A real-life story, it happened to me. I think, given our conversations this evening, that you might find it interesting. What about six o'clock tomorrow? Would you be free then?"

"That's good for us," said Daan, looking for confirmation from Boukje, who nodded. "So, until tomorrow."

The knock on the door came just after six and Liz welcomed their guests into La Tour. The wine and gin flowed, the wonderful olives Liz had discovered in the local market that morning were devoured, as Tom and Liz described their day exploring the village, and further afield along the river where they had had a picnic—classical French fare of cheese, baguette, olives and wine in the wonderful summer sun.

They were now sitting on a small terrace on an extension built to the side of La Tour, accessed through a door from its living area. Tom was in his usual 'I'm on holiday gear'—a pair of jogging bottoms, trainers and a baggy polo shirt which, if truth be told, had seen better days. Liz looked really comfortable too in a long, pale blue, cheesecloth dress, with several rows of her favourite bead necklaces, and light, leather sandals. She had never been a hippie but that evening, she could have easily been mistaken for one. The view across Chalabre to the foothills of the Pyrenees was quite stunning. The sun was warm and the early evening breeze balmy. With a robust red wine in hand and good company, what more could anyone want. *Perfection,* Tom thought to himself.

"So, your story, Tom?" said Daan. Boukje and Liz, deep in conversation, looked up together from across the small, round, wrought iron-and-tile table, towards Tom.

"OK. So, we're back in 1976," Tom said, settling to his task.

Chapter Four
September 1976

"Wonderful morning," he had said.

Tom looked up, "Beautiful."

"Do you mind?" said the blond, much-tanned, blue-eyed man, pointing to the seat next to him.

"Not at all, please do."

They were sitting on a park bench, looking across a grassy bank which sloped away to the Rhine, flowing steadily and glinting in the bright mid-afternoon sun, no more than fifty metres away. Nearby was a mobile snack bar or 'Schnell Imbiss'. This was Bonn, and behind them, arranged in orderly but uninspiring fashion, were the equally uninspiring, mostly dirty-white, modernist buildings of the West German Federal Government.

Tom was reading a file of papers. Their edges fluttered annoyingly in the breeze which periodically, and without warning, gusted across the grassy slope.

"Jeff Cogan," said the man, leaning forward with his right hand outstretched for Tom to shake, and shielding his eyes from the sun with his left.

"Tom, Tom Cooper." They shook hands. Tom noticed that this otherwise smart chap in a linen summer-suit and open-collared white shirt, had dirty fingernails. Tom always noticed incongruities like those. A girlfriend had once remarked that he was vainer than she was. *A hell of a claim,* Tom thought, given how long she spent in the bathroom each morning. At university, though, other good friends had teased him about Carly Simon's classic early-seventies hit, *You're So Vain.* It became a kind of anthem for his last two undergraduate years. Over the years, he had concluded that mirrors were probably the greatest, and simultaneously, the most annoying invention of the civilised world—and invented by a German in the mid-nineteenth century. In any event, he couldn't help but look, should he pass one.

"I was thinking of having a coffee," Cogan said, pointing to the snack bar. "You want one, perhaps?"

Tom closed his file. He wasn't going to finish the papers—that was clear, "Sure. Sounds good." They got up and walked the few steps to the little wagon.

"You are visiting, or maybe you work here?" Cogan asked.

"I'm doing some research. My PhD. I've just interviewed a senior civil-servant, about half-an-hour ago, and I also want to use the library over there," Tom pointed along the street that led away from the 'park-like area', where they were now standing.

"*Guten Tag*," said the girl behind the small counter.

"How do you take your coffee, Jeff?"

"Just black."

"*Zwei kaffee, bitte*," said Tom, "*Eine mit und eine ohne zahn.*"

"I'll get these," said Cogan. "So, what's your research about?"

As a relatively poor postgraduate research student, Tom didn't argue about being 'treated' to a coffee by a complete stranger. Instead, he launched into a well-rehearsed summary of the project. He had been asked the question so many times by people who weren't *really* interested, that he had learned to encapsulate the 80,000-word thesis into one bland sentence.

"I'm studying the way policies on 'gastarbeiter'—guest workers—were produced in the '50s, '60s and early-70s here, and comparing them to those on immigration to the UK over the same period." He waited for the usual 'Oh, yes, fascinating', and the quick change of subject.

"Guess the Brits have immigrants, and the Germans have 'guests', sums it up," Cogan replied, sipping the wonderful

22

coffee spoiled only by the polystyrene cup that it was served in.

Good God, someone who knows something about migration politics, Tom thought.

"Well, it's certainly part of the story. A lot more to it than that alone though." Tom was the expert here and, as always, he was determined to show it.

"Sure," Cogan replied without hesitation. "Guess the numbers are different too; not to mention the fact that it's the Turks who are the problem here and blacks who are your problem over there." The chat was moving onto familiar territory and Tom eased into it like pulling on an old shoe.

"Who is whose problem is a real debate that doesn't have the history here that it has in the UK. If you're black or a Turk, you're likely to see the government, your employer, or your landlord as the problem."

"When in Rome…and all that, though, it's never easy to accept different people, is it? They say, one in ten crimes committed here involves Turks. No time for 'em myself," Cogan said.

Here we go, thought Tom, *The same old sequence of events. It starts with something like a rational, balanced discussion. Then come the caveats, the 'my best friend is black but…' part of the conversation. If it goes further, the full array of stereotypes and prejudices will likely be on display.*

"Well, it takes all sorts, as my granddad used to say. So, what do you do, Jeff?" Tom had resorted to plan B; he would change the subject.

"I work at the American Embassy here."

"Thought I detected an American accent," Tom said. "How long have you been here?"

"Oh, about two years. Due to return to the States next year. A temporary tour of duty, part of the usual merry-go-round. Y'know, two years here, two years there. This department, then that."

"What do you do here? Oh sorry, perhaps I shouldn't ask that."

"No James Bond for sure. I just shuffle papers all day, apart from attending meetings, ambassador receptions, and the odd other party."

Tom looked at his watch as he drained his coffee.

"Well, sorry, my time's up. Better go. Could do to be in the library. It's been nice having a chat." Cogan finished his coffee.

"Listen," he said, "talking of parties, there's one at the Embassy tonight. Fancy coming along?"

Sounded great. Tom was staying on his own in a very small, characterless hotel on a side street, near the railway station. This evening would be like so many others. Writing up interview notes over a couple of beers in his room and then sitting in a bar eating bratwurst, chips and sauerkraut (or something equally cheap and unhealthy) whilst pretending to be interested in a book or some papers. Bed usually beckoned after the fourth beer.

"Well, er, well…" he looked down at his Chinos, soft slip-on shoes, polo shirt, and baggy linen jacket. "Haven't got any decent clothes. Y' know, travelling light. Pretty much just what I'm wearing now."

"No problem at all. It's just some local people, and some minor folk like me, from other embassies, for cheese and wine. It'll be very relaxed. Not an ambassador's reception. They're much more formal. Slacks and a shirt will be fine."

"Well… I mean…in that case, it would be great. Thanks very much. Where's the embassy? What time?"

Cogan fumbled in his inside jacket pocket and pulled out a small piece of paper and a pen, "Just let me know your hotel and I'll get a car to collect you. How does 7.30 sound?"

"Fine!" said Tom, jotting down the hotel name and street on the paper and handing it back to Cogan.

"That street is on my way back to the office. My car is in a carpark opposite the Kanzleramt. I could give you a lift back to town later. No problem at all."

"Thanks, that's a kind offer, but I'm not sure what time I'm leaving here," said Tom.

"I'll be finished here by five," Cogan said, "That's long enough for your work in the library, I bet? No need to pay the taxi fare. They're a rip-off, anyway."

Tom thought for a moment, as he checked his papers and put them inside his leather-look shoulder bag. Money was tight. He looked at his watch. It was almost four o'clock. An hour was plenty of time.

"OK. Many thanks. That will be great. Where should we meet?"

"Um? Outside the library? I can pull-in there."

"Great!"

Tom stood up and Cogan did too. Tom held out his hand.

"Tom, I wonder? Perhaps you would do *me* a favour?" Cogan lifted his briefcase from the park bench. "The Kanzleramt is a good walk from here, and I have a short meeting also in another ministry even further away. I don't need my case. Would you be able to keep it until we meet at five? Would save me carrying it around in this heat."

"Shouldn't be a problem," said Tom, "I'm only walking to the library just there. Are you sure it's OK? Y'know, embassy business and stuff?"

"No problem, Tom. It's locked. We'll see each other later anyway, and I have your hotel address in case you decide to run away with it." Cogan smiled and gave a small chuckle. Tom was reassured.

"Fine," he said, and took the case from Cogan. Tom picked up his shoulder bag, slung it over his shoulder and they walked together up the street, away from the park. They stood outside the library. Cogan handed Tom his case; they shook hands and with a 'see you at five', Cogan turned right towards the Kanzleramt. He waved briefly as he disappeared out of sight around a building. Tom mused on those turn of events.

Party at the embassy. Wow! Wait till I tell the folks about this. Could make some useful contacts. Who knows? Brilliant!

As he started to walk up the few steps of the library entrance, a small, camouflaged, armoured-car trundled slowly down the street behind him. He turned at the rumbling noise and deep throat of a powerful diesel engine. A soldier with earphones, full helmet and semi-automatic held diagonally in front of his chest, sat half-concealed on top. The soldier scanned side-to-side in a deliberate but almost-nonchalant way. He saw Tom but didn't interrupt his side-to-side scanning of the area.

Tom stood rooted to the spot. He had seen this, or a similar 'mini tank' earlier in the day, near the entrance to the government complex. He'd seen two foot-soldiers at the barriers to the Kanzleramt also bristling with the hardware of war. He'd thought little of it then. After all, this was 1976. It was the time of the *Rote Armee Fraktion* (the Red Army Faction), its founders: Andreas Baader and Ulrike Meinhof— the latter-day Bonnie and Clyde, who had terrorised half of Europe and held West Germany to ransom with murders, kidnappings and bombing. He had thought nothing of the security this morning, but now...

He looked down at the maroon, Antler-type briefcase in his hand. He looked at the rear of the armoured car, now well passed him and trundling on its way.

Oh my God, he thought.

"Fucking hell," he said out loud.

A young woman came through the library doors and down the few steps towards him. Tom smiled.

"Tag," he said a little nervously.

"Guten Tag," she said briskly, bristling at his use of the more familiar greeting. She brushed passed him, turned right and disappeared along the main street in the direction the mini-tank had come from. Tom walked up the six steps towards the library doors and stopped in front of them.

Christ, what do I do now? he said to himself. *C'mon, get a grip. Now think this through.*

Look. You're meeting the guy at five. You know he works at the American Embassy. If this is a bomb, then why give it to you? Blow up the library? What the hell for? Kill you and some German civil servants for sure and show that anyone can get access to government buildings and set a bomb? Yeh, but if it is a bomb, it must be timed. He couldn't be sure he'd find someone stupid like you to act as his mule. Perhaps, he didn't need to. Perhaps, he would have done it himself. Right. This is stupid.

"Too many spy films in your head, Cooper," he muttered.

Tom went into the library. It was 4.10 pm. He was sure this wasn't a bomb. It didn't add up. No bomber would risk an unknown courier. In any event, they must surely have security screening in the library. The case would be scanned.

There was no scanner, or if there was, he couldn't see it, and in any event, no one stopped him to check his bags. Of course, they didn't. They knew him from his several earlier visits.

"*Guten tag, Herr Cooper,*" said the rather lovely looking and lovely sounding young woman at the front desk. He returned the greeting but moved on swiftly—more quickly than he wanted, or that he had done before.

He sat at a small desk on which he put some of his papers, left his bags on his chair, and went to seek out the records he was looking for that day. He found them fairly easily and after scanning through the folders, he selected some key pages and copied them on the public photocopier. It was now 4.50 pm. Time to go.

Tom stood at the library entrance and watched each car that passed. It was then 5.30 pm and Cogan had not shown. He could feel the tension grow within him, reminding him of all those Saturday afternoons when just a small boy, he waited for the end of a horse race which he was watching with his granddad. Six o'clock and still no sign of Cogan. He looked at the briefcase standing on the pavement beside him.

At that moment, Tom was overcome by a mixture of irresistible curiosity and crass stupidity. He was Tom Cooper, BA (Hons), MSc in Social Science, researching for his PhD, but for the next few minutes, he was to be Tom Cooper, village idiot; a person with one brain cell which was malfunctioning. Cogan had said the briefcase was locked but nevertheless, 'village idiot Cooper' bent down, laid the briefcase on its back and placed his thumbs on the slide release catches.

Click!

The case was certainly not locked.

Tom had heard the expressions: 'his heart was in his mouth', 'his chest thumped like a drum'. There were many variations on the same theme. He now knew all of them were rubbish. It was his head that was pounding, not his chest. His stomach pitched and tossed like a small boat in a storm. He felt sure his eyes were standing on stalks about three feet from his face.

He bent over the case. The small latches were open, standing to attention like privates on parade. He lifted the top of the case very, very slowly. Half an inch, an inch, two inches. Then, quite involuntarily, he lifted the lid fully open.

"Bitte' Frau Schaeffer. Ich brauche der telefon nummer das American Embassy," he said with a shaking voice. Whether his German was grammatically correct, he had no idea, and he cared even less. He just needed that number.

"Bitte," said the wizened, stony-faced woman, as she passed the telephone directory to him across the small front desk of the hotel, and a few moments later, also the telephone. He knew the call would be charged at an exorbitant rate and added to his bill, but that was unimportant just now.

"Hello, yes, er… I'm trying to contact Jeff Cogan, who works in the embassy. Yes, that's right. Jeff Cogan. I see. Are you sure? OK. Oh, can you tell me, is there a party at the embassy tonight? Right. OK. Thank you. Thanks for your help."

Tom sat on the side of the bed. It was now just after 6.30 pm. Tom knew that Jeff Cogan was very unlikely to arrive, nor would any car from the embassy be calling for him. Jeff Cogan didn't work at the embassy and there wasn't a party there that night either. Apparently, there had been one last Friday, and there was a formal reception next Monday. This was Thursday. The case lay open beside him on the bed. Tom reached for his beer, gulped back half the bottle and looked again at the case.

It was a very warm, sultry, late summer evening, but the sweat which ran down his left temple had nothing to do with the temperature in his shabby little room. He was recalling the moment on the steps of the library as he stared in disbelief at the open case. Disbelief not about what was inside the case, but the fact that he had opened it at all?

"Y'know, Cooper? You're bloody bonkers," he said out loud to himself, "You deserve to be locked up and the key thrown away." This was a favourite expression of his mother, who used it frequently about anyone who was in her words 'daft'. He leant across and examined again the contents of the case, now displayed in an orderly row on the bed.

When the lid on the case was fully open for the first time on the library steps, Tom had his eyes shut. The absurd thought that this might somehow save him from a bomb blast, almost certainly powerful enough to have dismembered him, had not crossed his mind. It was, just as the final act of opening the case had been, quite involuntary. When the blast didn't come, he opened his eyes, expecting to see a collection of papers, perhaps a diary, and some pens—the typical paraphernalia of a civil servant or manager. What he saw was a sheaf of lined A4 paper, a brown shoelace, a paperclip, a pencil and a small hard-backed book.

He picked up the book again. *Robur der Eroberer* by Jules Verne—German Language Edition—bound in a tan-coloured leather-effect cover. He flicked through the pages just as he had done in the back of the taxi from the library to the hotel. He once again held the book by its front and back cover, spreading them outwards, and shook the book hard. Just as in the taxi, nothing fell from the pages.

There was nothing to examine of the shoelace, the paperclip and the pencil. They were, after all, just a shoelace, a paperclip and a pencil. The A4 paper was blank. It looked new. Under the dim light of the bedside lamp, he looked for impression marks in the hope that something had been written on a top sheet which was now missing. Nothing. Tom got up from the bed, drank the rest of his bottle of beer and opened another one. No such luxury as a fridge in this room, so the beer spurted out all over him. He hated warm beer but tonight, it would have to do.

"Any port in a storm," he muttered to himself. He paced the room, bottle in hand, trying to figure out what the hell was going on.

He had, by now, examined the case thoroughly. No name tags. Nothing in the several small pockets in the lid. No false bottom—well, not as far as he could tell. There was so much that just didn't add up.

Jeff Cogan, or whatever his real name was, didn't work for the American Embassy. Sure, he had an American accent. Well, of sorts. It was tinged with something else though: Swedish, Danish or even German, perhaps. Tom had thought this when they were chatting on the bench. Then, it seemed unimportant. An insignificant detail. Now, it seemed potentially significant, though he didn't know why. Also, Cogan's fingernails were dirty. In fact, very dirty. Odd for an office worker. This was another thing which had crossed his mind at the time, but despatched as quickly as the accent in the thrill of being invited to an embassy party. Why should someone dump a briefcase on someone else, especially when it contained such rubbish?

"If you want a courier," Tom said out loud, "you must want him to carry something important. Or you've nicked the case, taken out anything of value and want rid." Tom sat on the bed, "In that case, then dump the bloody thing in the Rhine or a waste bin, or under a parked car."

"And another thing," said Tom, as if speaking to an audience, "How did he know I spoke English?" To his knowledge, Tom hadn't spoken English to anyone for three days, except briefly in an interview with a senior civil servant in the Ministry for Employment. By now, Tom's beer had been despatched. He put the bottle onto the bedside table and looked again at the case.

Nothing for it, he thought.

"Frau Schaeffer, konnen sie mir sagen in welche richtung liegt der Polizei hier in Bonn?" Tom's German was very far from perfect. He had attended three lunchtime sessions at the

30

Goethe Institute in Manchester before leaving for West Germany. Before that, he could say *'ja und nein'*. After the classes, he could say '*Mein name* is Tom Cooper'; *'ja'* und *'nein'*. Most of the language he now had, he had learned in Germany by watching old American movies or British sitcoms with subtitles on the TV and practising on friends and unsuspecting shop assistants. He had learned most from Monika, the German woman he had fallen in love with in Manchester, when he worked for the Home Office, and with whom he now lived in an apartment on the edge of Bremen. Despite her best efforts, his German tended to be pretty colloquial. He wasn't at all sure of tenses and related grammar. Anyway, everyone seemed to understand what he was saying…more-or-less.

"The Police Station, Herr Cooper?" she said, "What is the problem?"

Tom proceeded to explain, as best he could, in German, and with appropriate brevity, what had happened. By the time he was on the steps of the library with the case, the grey-haired stony-faced Frau Schaeffer, looked and sounded, for all the world, like a Nun on 'speed'.

"Mein Gott! Mein Gott!"

"Gott in Himmel!"

The frequency and speed of her 'crossings' was too much for the naked eye to take in. All-the-more-so as it was done whilst lifting the telephone receiver and dialling. Frau Schaeffer could make a fortune as a circus juggler, Tom thought, as she handed him the phone and disappeared, 'crossing herself' furiously, into the room behind the front desk, closing the door firmly behind her. Frau Schaeffer hadn't waited to work out that the case didn't contain a bomb. If it had, Tom wouldn't be relaying the story to her now. The terror campaign of recent years had had its desired effect on decent, god-fearing citizens, like her.

The directions to the police station provided by the man on the end of the telephone convinced Tom to walk there.

The fresh evening air will do me good, he thought to himself, *and the walk too. Probably help me get my thoughts together.* The walk took him about 40 minutes, and he did feel refreshed by it. Seeing people going about their everyday business, travelling home from work, or going out for the evening certainly had brought him down to earth… Well, for the time being.

Chapter Five
September 1976

Tom stood in front of a wire cage. He pressed the small bell. Beyond the wire-mesh door was another normal door. A moment later, the mesh door opened, and he walked into the cage.

"What do you want?" said a disembodied voice through the loudspeaker.

"I spoke to someone earlier on the telephone about a briefcase I have been given."

There was a pause and the second door opened.

The officer on the desk asked again what he wanted and Tom reported his earlier telephone conversation about the briefcase.

"Please wait a moment," said the officer, pointing to a seat opposite the desk.

Tom sat down, leaning forward, forearms resting on his knees, hands clasped in front of him. To the right across the small waiting area sat a crumpled heap of humanity. A longhaired, dishevelled, possibly young man who looked completely 'spaced-out'. *Booze or dope, or both,* Tom thought.

He looked down at the briefcase sitting innocently on the floor between his feet.

What would the police make of his story? What if there were some 'secrets' hidden in the case or in the book? How could he explain them?

"*Herr Cooper?*" The voice came from behind him to his right.

"*Ja,*" said Tom, standing up quickly but with the briefcase still between his feet.

"Please come this way." The officer beckoned him through the door to the right of the desk and down a corridor. The officer opened the door into a small room on the left. Another man was already there, seated at a table.

"Herr Cooper," said the man at the table. "Please have a seat." Tom sat down, placing the briefcase across his knees and facing the man across the table. Another officer entered the room and sat down a little way from the table with a notebook on his knee.

"First, Herr Cooper, perhaps you would provide us with some personal information?" said the officer, who had just entered the room, in slow and deliberately articulated German.

"No problem," said Tom, realising by now that the interview was probably going to be in German and hoping his was up to it.

"Thank you, Herr Cooper. Your German is very good. So, can you now tell me the events that led to you obtaining this briefcase?" said the first officer, who, by now, had a lot of Tom's life history in his little notebook. Tom began to relate the events of the day. It was now well past nine pm. He was feeling knackered but excited. The words tumbled out of his mouth like water gushing from a tap. A stream of consciousness, as some might say. He hadn't gone very far when the man at the table interrupted him.

"Please, please, slowly. Take your time. Describe Jeff Cogan for us."

"Er…well, short, blond hair, blue eyes. He was wearing a white, opened-collared shirt and a linen suit. He—"

"How tall, how old?" asked the first officer. Tom hadn't thought about either of these.

"I guess he was…well…perhaps… I'd say late-30s, maybe 40. About five feet 11, or maybe six feet."

"Metres. How much in metres?" asked the man at the table in a somewhat irritated tone.

34

Tom counted himself as a good European. However, his brain had steadfastly resisted all attempts to work in metric. Shopping was much hit and miss. He regularly found himself with enough ham to feed an army battalion, despite needing only enough for a sandwich lunch for a few days. How much *was* a kilo, anyway? And buying clothes? Well, sizing was a complete mystery. And metres and centimetres were not very far behind.

"Well, you see, er…sorry…but I don't know." The two policemen glanced knowingly at each other. Tom felt a prat.

"Stand up!" said the officer with the notebook. Tom stood, fearing the tone in the officer's voice.

"How tall compared to you, for example?" he said, raising his hand towards the top of Tom's head.

"Ah," Tom said with some relief, "about this tall." He raised his right hand, palm downwards, three or four inches above his head.

"Good. Very good. And did he have any special features? Rings? Tattoos? Scars?" said the man at the table, who was now, in fact, standing near the door.

"Yes, he had dirty fingernails."

"What?"

"He had dirty fingernails. As if he had been gardening or working on his car or something like that."

"And anything else?"

Tom scratched the side of his head. *Yes, he did. He did!!!* he thought to himself excitedly. "He had a small mark above his right cheek," Tom pointed to his right temple. He didn't know the German word for 'temple'. He guessed the German for 'church' wouldn't be quite right somehow.

"It was a small, round mark. I can draw it for you," he said enthusiastically.

"No problem, Herr Cooper. I believe I know what you mean," said the officer scribbling in the notebook.

The man near the door moved back towards the table.

"So, to the briefcase," he said, stretching forward across the table towards Tom. Tom slid it to him, handle first.

"We will take this and examine it, Herr Cooper," he said. He didn't open it. "Thank you for giving us the information. You look tired. We have no more questions and I think you should get some sleep."

"But, but…what happens now? Don't you want to look inside? What do *you* think this is about?" Tom was tired— knackered in fact—but he was desperate for someone, *anyone,* to explain these bizarre events.

"My guess is that this man stole the case and used you to get it off his hands," said the officer with the notebook. His colleague nodded.

"Anyway, we will look at the case carefully. If no one claims it within three months, it is yours to keep." There was so much Tom wanted to say, but his disbelief was only matched by the total failure of his brain to work his mouth properly. He left the police station, escorted outside by the note-taker and wandered back to his hotel.

The following morning, he checked out of the hotel as planned, paying the bill, including what he had guessed would be an exorbitant amount for the one local phone call he had made. Frau Schaeffer gave him a receipt, thanked him rather abruptly, and wished him well—also rather abruptly. Tom thought that if she could have pushed him out the front door on roller skates, then she would have done.

His journey north to the flat he shared with his partner, Monika von Strauss, was completely uneventful—which meant he could rest on the train and try to recover from the events of the last couple of days. When he arrived home, Monika was out and had left a note to say she was taking an extra class in gymnastics at the school. Although she was a teacher of English at the nearby gymnasium, or grammar school as it would be called in the UK, she was also an accomplished gymnast and often took extra-curricular classes or even, sometimes, gymnastics during the timetabled PE lessons. They had met in Manchester where Tom worked for a while doing social research for the government.

Monika was on a routine summer vacation to England which she did every year, mainly to make sure her use of

36

colloquial English was up-to-date for her students back in Germany. She and Tom met at a BBQ party some of her friends were having—and it turned out one of them was a friend of Tom's too. She had known Dave and Sally for a few years and visited them every summer. Tom had only met Dave this year when they both worked on the same research project. Monika's summer vacation this year was going to be anything but routine. At the end of it, Tom had decided to quit his job and move to Germany to live with her and, he hoped, do fieldwork for his PhD if the university accepted his application. In all sorts of respects, these were to be life-changing decisions.

Monika came home about 6.30 and Tom proceeded to tell her all about his experiences in Bonn. Monika had no better explanation for 'the briefcase affair' as she called it, than the Bonn police had suggested. They chatted about it for a good time before and during supper and then over a fair few more glasses of wine before Tom became so tired, he just had to go to bed. Monika had been expecting a more romantic homecoming, but she could see he was almost completely exhausted and good for nothing except sleeping.

Just over three months later, he woke abruptly to the sound of ringing in his ears. He looked at the alarm clock. It was silent. *The doorbell,* he thought. Monika was not in bed beside him and so must be already at school. No doubt she had left at her usual time, seven am, to be at school for the start of lessons at eight o'clock. He hadn't heard anything of her showering, dressing and leaving. She was good at knowing when he needed the sleep. He dragged himself out of bed, slipped into his bathrobe and stumbled along the corridor to their front door. As he opened it, he was greeted by a blast of icy cold air coming in through the open outside door to the apartment block and sight of the man who had left it ajar.

"A parcel for you, Herr Cooper. Please sign here."

Tom took the small pad from the young man and scribbled a signature. He took the parcel, handed the pad back to the postman who gave him the top copy, said thanks and Tom closed the door.

That morning, Tom found himself looking every few minutes at the briefcase sitting innocently on the dining-come-study table. It had arrived well-packaged, but with no letter, not even a short note. The parcel had come from the police in Bonn, according to the postmark. Inside the case was the sheaf of lined A4 paper, the brown shoelace, the pencil, the paperclip and the hard-backed book.

Chapter Six
July 2001

"So, what do you think it was about, Tom?" Boukje asked.

"Well," Tom said, "To be honest, I have never come to a better answer than the Bonn police." However, even as he said this, another event in his life suddenly popped into Tom's head. As Daan began to outline several possible sequences of cause and effect to explain the curious events in Bonn, Tom was somewhere else altogether.

"Tom? Tom!" Liz said with an urgency, "Boukje's asking you about the briefcase."

"Oh. Er, sorry, Boukje," Tom burbled, "Well, no, I don't have it any longer. Left it in Germany. I have the book and that's all."

Tom poured more wine for everyone. The Fitou he had bought from the local 'Huit a Huit' just a few minutes from 'La Tour' was really quite superb. Less than half the price such a wine would have cost in the UK. "Bloody disgrace what we pay for wine," Tom muttered to himself.

"You were miles away then, Tom, what are you thinking about?" said Liz.

"My trip to Belfast," said Tom, still a little distant.

"That was when you stayed with some people you'd met on holiday, wasn't it?" asked Liz, handing round some of the nibbles.

"Yes, Jack and Myra. Met them in Corfu," Tom replied.

"Another story I think, Boukje," said Daan.

"Well, we must hear this too," said Boukje, settling into the unusually comfortable foldaway 'director's chair' and looking genuinely excited. Liz topped-up the wine, mixed a couple of fresh 'G&Ts' and glanced at Tom. This story was about a time before she had met Tom. He had met Jack and Myra on holiday with his first wife. That was certainly very much in the past from Tom's point of view. His life with Liz was brilliant and he loved her very much. Tom glanced up and realised Liz was also keen to hear the story again. Somehow, it seemed more exciting now.

"All right," said Tom, "But this time, you need to go back to 1987."

"Like being in a time machine, all this dodging between decades," Daan said.

"Quiet, Daan. Let's hear the story," Boukje said impatiently.

Chapter Seven
October 1987

The line of passengers moved steadily, if quite slowly, through the security-and-passport check. Tom was immediately aware of the soldier with an automatic rifle standing behind the official who was checking passports and landing cards. To the right of the soldier was a sombre and serious-looking 'suit'. *Special Branch,* thought Tom.

He handed his passport and landing card to the official. Barely a second or two later, his passport was being examined by 'the suit'.

"Where are you staying?" said the official. Tom gave Jack's address, but thought it a curious, even dumb question, as the address was on his landing card.

"On holiday or business?" said 'the suit' flatly, but Tom thought with a faintly aggressive tone.

"Holiday. Visiting friends."

Tom walked out of Arrivals and saw Jack and Myra waving frantically. It was good to see them again. They had been great company on the holiday, and though they had had little contact since then, Tom had no reason to believe they would now be any different.

"Sorry to hear about the divorce, Tom," said Myra. "Must have been some tough times for you both." Tom had given them a brief summary of the divorce when he phoned them to arrange the visit. He had to, really, given his first wife wouldn't be joining him on the trip.

"Sure, but mainly sorting out who got what from the old house, the car, etc. In the end, we both got what we deserved, I suppose, in more ways than one. Still, I cannot help but wonder, sometimes, about the settlement. It's all history now and I've moved on, Myra."

The rest of the day was taken up with catching-up. Jack and Myra had a small semi in a supposedly 'mixed' area of the city. This was difficult for Tom to imagine: the kerbstones of their street were painted red, white and blue and the union flag flew from every other telegraph pole and street lamp. A 'mixed' area? Whatever the outward appearance, Jack explained to Tom that there *were* those who supported a united Ireland living next door, to those who were staunch unionists right along the street. There were even families in the same house who were split down the middle on this most-crucial-of-all definers of people in this part of the world.

Sunday arrived on time, but Tom didn't. Drinking into the early hours with Jack, who had a capacity for alcohol—and recovery from it—the equal or better of Dean Martin, had left its mark. For his part, Jack sat at the breakfast table in the kitchen as if he'd been on a health farm for a week—though his waistline told a different story. Jack and Myra had decided it would be good to visit the folk museum on the edge of Belfast. Proud of their twin heritages—Britain and Ireland—they wanted Tom to see something of the special features of Ulster's history.

Jack had an irresistible and infectious sense of humour. Like the best of the 'new comedians' of the eighties and later, he came at the world from a different direction than most people. Every day, mundane conversation became an event in Jack's company, made even more hilarious by the deep Belfast accent in which he retold them. Tom's stomach ached before they were even halfway to the museum. They were all in good form. The small, silver escort slowed behind a long queue of traffic.

"Checkpoint," said Jack dryly.

Two hundred yards ahead, Tom could see from the passenger seat a grey, partly-camouflaged Land Rover and a soldier with an automatic rifle, positioned diagonally across his chest, directing the odd car into a coned 'runoff' area at the side of the road. The queue moved steadily forward. Very few vehicles were being pulled over, but as they slowly approached the Land Rover, the soldier peered closely into the car and signalled Jack into the inspection area.

"Bloody amazing," he muttered.

"What?" said Tom.

"Lived all my life in Belfast and never been pulled over at a checkpoint. Now, with our guest, and I get it."

The soldier demanded ID. Tom gave his passport. The soldier asked Jack where they were heading. He examined the passes carefully, peered into the car looking at ID photos and the real versions in turn. He walked around the car and clearly noted the registration.

"What the bloody hell was that all about?" shouted Myra, as they left the inspection lane and re-joined the queue.

"Bloody amazing. No idea. Must be Tom here. You haven't done anything bad in England, have you, Tom? Are you on the run?" Jack laughed uproariously as he said this. They all laughed together with Tom's, "certainly not," drowned by the noise.

The folk museum was splendid. Reconstructed houses and shops from Ulster's past with most of them occupied by people in costumes of the appropriate period doing the things people of that time would have done in the ways they would have done them. It reminded Tom of the village at Ironbridge, near Telford, and he thought it similar in many ways to the Beamish Museum in County Durham.

They had a full day at the museum, including a pub lunch. Jack and Tom had a couple of beers, so Myra drove home. By the time they got there, Tom was pretty tired and retired early—well, at least by Jack's standards.

Jack and Myra wanted Tom to see the centre of Belfast, so the following day, it was planned that he and Jack would go there by bus.

"So you two lads can have a jar or two," Myra had said in her Northern Irish drawl and a hug and a wink for Jack. There were two other reasons for this.

The first and necessary reason for the bus trip was that Myra had to go to work and needed the car. The case load of a social worker respected neither weekends nor visitors from England. The second, as Myra explained, was that it would allow Tom to see more of the city as the bus meandered its way to the centre. The third reason, completely unnecessary but at least as important as the other two in Jack's eyes, was that Tom had to visit the Crown Bar and sample not only its atmosphere, but also its Guinness. According to Jack, Sir John Betjeman—onetime Poet Laureate—had called it 'The Queen of Bars'. Even had the car been available, driving was not sensible.

The journey into town did give Tom a chance to see a few sights. One was a police station, fortified seemingly against all-comers, with whatever weapons modern urban, warfare could muster. It was definitely not a police station in any sense that Tom could understand. With this image still firmly in mind, Tom saw the bus approach massive wrought-iron gates. Beyond them, Royal Avenue was lined either side by all the shops of a typical British High Street. It was crowded. This was the city centre.

The gates swung open to let the bus through. At the far end of the street were sister gates, opening and closing to let traffic out on to Donegal Place. In later years, reflecting on his trip, Tom saw the gates opening and closing in a macabre ballet—a sort of metaphor for 'the troubles' in that part of Ireland over so many years. His English Literature teacher would have been proud of him.

Jack and Tom meandered up the main street towards City Hall. A magnificent building, which sat serenely behind a large square. City Hall looked for all the world as if it was the seat of a stable government in a land of plenty; neither of which, sadly, were true at this time. As Tom admired the view, Jack grabbed his arm and directed him to the right and into the Crown Bar.

Tom soaked up the atmosphere—and the Guinness. After his second, this was certainly 'The Queen of Bars'. Even before the glow of calm joy which now filled him—as it always did after drinking quality Guinness—Tom had

44

realised this was a special place to be. He resolved to return one day.

Sumptuous dark wood interspersed with bright stained glass and Victorian tiles lit carefully by old-fashioned lamps; snug cubicles with bells to summon a waiter were occupied by small groups in private conversation; the open bar area buzzed with lively banter. For a while, Tom was preoccupied by the work of the barmen. As each order was taken, new glasses of Guinness would join those already lined up across the bar, each at various stages in the lifecycle of a perfect glass of Guinness: from the agitated creamy-brown infant, right through to the cocoa-coloured adolescent, to the smooth ebony and ivory adult. The barmen always knew whose glass was ready, and you didn't get it until it *was* ready.

Tom began to realise that this way of serving Guinness was much more than a process required by the physical properties of the drink. It reflected and was part of a culture built on the belief that everything worthwhile takes time. 'Relax and enjoy' took on a new meaning for Tom. This was a friendly, warm, totally beguiling place. Sadly though, the time came to head home. They went out with Jack leading the way to where the bus would stop. It was raining, not heavily, more a steady drizzle which can soak the most resilient outerwear. So, they sheltered inside the large doorway of a shop opposite the bus stop.

One or more camouflaged Land Rovers passed slowly by several times. After a while, one stopped and disgorged its occupants.

They approached purposefully. The leading soldier asked firmly for their 'ID'. No sooner had he opened Tom's passport than Tom found himself turned violently around, his face pressed hard against the plate-glass window of the shop doorway with hands running up and down his body feverishly but deliberately.

In another moment, he was spun around again, a semi-automatic now pointing directly at his face. Tom could see Jack to his left, not two yards away—with a second soldier's semi-automatic virtually caressing his right cheek. Jack stood upright and rigid. Tom was scared and curious, but the full realisation of his situation had yet to dawn on him.

Without a word, another soldier, a sergeant, came towards them from the Land Rover. He spoke briefly to the two soldiers guarding Jack and Tom. The guns never wavered from their duty and were putting the fear of God into both of them.

"What the hell is going on?" Tom whispered to Jack. "We haven't done anything. I'm going to ask what—"

"You'll do no such thing," Jack asserted quietly but forcefully.

"Answer questions, don't ask them. You can be banged-up for days here for no apparent reason. Just answer all the questions."

The guns remained motionless.

"Where are you staying in Belfast," the sergeant asked Tom in a steady but pointed manner.

"At his place," said Tom, moving his right hand to point at Jack.

The semi-automatic pointing at him clicked again. Tom froze completely this time.

"Keep still," said the sergeant looking at Jack, who provided the address.

"How long are you staying in Belfast?"

"Four days."

"Business or pleasure?"

"Visiting my friends so it's pleasure, of course."

"Another answer like that and you'll be on your way to a nice, cosy cell."

The sergeant moved closer to Tom.

"What is your address in England? What do you do for a living? Where do you work?"

After he had answered, the sergeant returned to the Land Rover. This time, Tom could see the soldier in the Land Rover talking, under instruction, into a huge 'walkie-talkie'.

The semi-automatic hadn't moved an inch, but to Tom, the barrel seemed bigger and closer than ever before. He began to shiver. He was wet and it was cold, but this was the shiver of fear. Blind, growing, panic-stricken fear. The sergeant came back.

"How long have you lived at your present address?"

"About two years."

"Have you lived anywhere else in Lancaster?"

"Yes, in a village called Halton."

"Do you belong to a political party?"

"No."

"Have you ever been a member of a political party?"

"Yes. I was a member of the Labour Party when I lived in Hertfordshire."

"What are you planning to do whilst you are in Belfast?"

"Have a few drinks, meet some of his friends and see the city. I don't really know."

"Why were you standing in this shop doorway?"

"Sheltering from the rain while we waited for a bus."

"What number bus?"

"I don't know, but he…" Tom nodded towards Jack.

"A 58," said Jack.

The sergeant went back to the Land Rover and this time had a lengthy conversation with the soldier who had the walkie-talkie. He seemed to also have conversations with someone on the other end.

The semi-automatics remained trained on their faces. Motionless.

The sergeant came back.

"Stay exactly where you are until we are in the Land Rover and are on our way. Do not move a muscle. These soldiers have orders to shoot if you do. And they don't miss."

The sergeant walked steadily backwards towards the Land Rover. He was followed, also backwards, by the two soldiers wielding the guns—which remained steadfastly pointing towards them. They slid one by one into the Land Rover and left.

Tom stood motionless. Jack fumbled in his coat pocket and retrieved his mobile phone. He was shaking—with cold and fear—and it took three attempts to successfully dial the number.

"It's me."

"Where the hell have you been? I've—"

"You'll not believe what has happened. We are OK but we'll be late. Best if you call Pat and tell him to meet us at the pub in Carnmoney rather than at his house. I'll explain everything. Bye."

Jack switched-off the mobile phone and stood shaking, looking at Tom. Tom was trying to say something but nothing came from his lips. His brain wasn't operating properly and his mouth, dry as a bone, wasn't cooperating anyway.

Jack tried to hail a taxi. The bus had long gone. *Curious,* Tom thought, *these bloody empty taxis aren't stopping.*

"They've seen what has just gone on," said Jack, almost throwing himself under yet another empty 'For Hire' taxi speeding by. Eventually, a taxi *did* stop. Tom sank thankfully into the back seat.

Chapter Eight
July 2001

"That's another frightening story, Tom," said Boukje.

"It is, but I don't see the connection with the briefcase incident," said Daan, finishing the last olive.

"Well, that possibility has only just occurred to me, to be honest," said Tom. "You see, about three months after I left Belfast, I had a really weird phone call from Myra and I now wonder about what she said."

"What was it?" said Liz.

That call had been about Myra and Jack's astonishment at seeing Tom's double on a news item on BBC 2, Northern Ireland. On hearing this, Tom had immediately tried BBC 2 on his own television in his house in Lancaster, but it was a different programme to that showing in Northern Ireland.

"He's exactly like you, Tom," Myra had said. "He's wanted by the police. He's connected to the IRA and only been out of The Maze for a couple of months. It explains everything that happened when you were here."

"What was his name?" asked Daan.

"Declan Brophy."

"And you think the briefcase in Bonn was meant for him, eh, Tom?" Daan poured the remainder of the wine. Tom didn't answer. He was deep in thought.

The journey back to the UK went as planned. They had a wonderful time eating in brilliant restaurants, walking in beautiful countryside, exploring markets and so many small, local shops in small villages that it was impossible to remember even half of them. When they crossed on the ferry, the car boot was full of various wines and other 'things' bought in the myriad of small shops—chosen mostly by Liz, Tom later recalled.

As they unpacked back at Fairholme, Tom was already thinking more about the two tales and how they might be connected, than the great holiday they had just had, the mountain of post-lying on the hall floor or the nineteen messages flashing on the answerphone.

Chapter Nine
November 2001

Four months ago, as they left La Tour after a wonderfully relaxing stay, Tom had asked Daan if he could find out anything about Declan Brophy. Tom thought that being a retired journalist who had worked in Amsterdam and the USA covering European affairs, Daan might have sources who were still well-connected. Brophy was Tom's Provisional IRA lookalike. Lookalike wasn't really in it. Tom had been stunned when he first saw a picture of Brophy from the Irish Times sent to him by Jack. It was almost like looking in a mirror.

Daan had uncovered some basic and some not-so-basic information from his old hack-friends. Brophy was two years younger than Tom. Born in Antrim, he had graduated from Queen's University in 1971, with first-class honours in Financial Management and Accounting. He had not been politically active at university—well, publicly at least—but some of his friends were known IRA sympathisers. After Queen's, Brophy had worked for a medium-sized and very respectable firm of accountants and financial consultants in Belfast. It was in 1974 that his name was first linked with the Provos. Documents obtained by an undercover agent in Boston, USA, referred to Brophy acting to secure offshore investments linked to both, the IRA and through various 'shell companies' to the Mafia. Brophy was an IRA 'suit'. There had never been any evidence that he had held a gun, let alone killed anyone—at least, not directly.

Brophy had been banged-up in The Maze in 1979—coincidentally, the year Tom started fulltime teaching—found guilty of conspiring with others to import illegal firearms and explosives into Northern Ireland. The haul was worth just over £4 million.

"Rumour had it at the time," said Daan, on a poor line from France, "that Brophy had been betrayed by some powerful players in the Provisionals."

"Why?" asked Tom.

"Nothing certain," said Daan, "but Harris, an old buddy in the States, reckons Brophy let them down badly earlier in the seventies. Failed to deliver on a big deal or something like that. Nothing came out at the trial, but Harris is sure he was, as they say, 'grassed-up'."

Since that conversation, Tom had been trawling through back-microfilm copies of all the main national newspapers published in Ireland, the UK and the US between 1974 and 1978. Nothing about Declan Brophy (except his arrest and trial), nothing about a big deal involving him going belly-up in Ireland, Northern Ireland, Germany or anywhere else.

Tom woke to the smell of bacon cooking. He swung his legs slowly out of bed and sat staring out of the window. Blue sky as far as the eye could see. Palms facing him, he rubbed each eye with the heel of each hand—the ritual and regularly vain attempt to encourage his brain to catch up with his body on waking. He slipped into jogging bottoms, t-shirt and trainers and padded through to the small en-suite. He glanced in the mirror over the hand basin. Not a pretty sight.

"You look bloody awful," he said out loud, "You'll frighten the punters."

Tom and Liz lived in a three-storey Victorian-end terrace. Liz had wanted to run a bed-and-breakfast for years and two years ago, when they bought Fairholme, came her chance. There had been some remodelling needed in the house and some repairs, but it worked beautifully as both, their home and a B&B. Liz had developed a thriving small business in less than two years. The books were as full as either of them wanted or needed. The business website was superb and enquiries came from all over the world. Last night and that night, they had Ed and Helen, a couple from the US (on recommendation) and Sasha and Frank, a younger couple from London. As Tom came down the final flight of stairs, he could hear Liz chatting with the guests in the dining room about various places to see in the city.

Tom made himself a cup of tea amidst the clutter of a small kitchen that had just delivered four, full English breakfasts and all the trimmings. He sat at the table in the breakfast room which was open-plan to the kitchen, cradling his mug of tea in both hands, trying desperately to waken up properly.

"Hello, my darling," said Liz brightly, as she appeared through the door from the dining room. "You'll never guess. Those four had never met until this morning, but it seems they have a common friend. Ed and Helen have a close friend in Manchester who has a brother in London. Sasha and Frank know the brother really well—he's the boyfriend of Sasha's best friend from school. Amazing or what?"

"Hm," said Tom, "Amazing." As usual, he'd heard the words tumbling from Liz's mouth, but his brain hadn't yet translated them into meaningful sentences.

"My darling isn't awake yet, I think."

Tom required at least two mugs of tea, two cigarettes (outside in the small courtyard—the B&B was fully no-smoking) and a strong cup of coffee to be *fully* awake. Thirty minutes later, all requirements had been met, he'd even helped Liz clear the dishes from breakfast and they sat together at the breakfast room table.

"I'm giving up this stupid search, Liz," Tom said flatly, "There's no connection between Brophy, me and the briefcase. It was just coincidence after all."

Liz studied Tom. She knew him well enough to know that he was convincing himself of this apparent 'fact' and what he really wanted was for someone—Liz preferably—to convince him otherwise.

"You're really tired, Tom. Why don't you rest this morning, read the papers or whatever, I've got to go into town. I've to service the rooms. When I get back, we can go through it all together."

"OK," said Tom, without any real enthusiasm.

The rest of the morning passed by with Tom reading the sports pages, drinking coffee, having the odd cigarette, changing a light bulb, emptying the waste bins and generally doing nothing much at all. He mulled over 'the search' briefly from time to time.

Liz prepared some sandwiches with their favourite smoked ham from Franco's Deli—the best in town by a mile as far as they were concerned. They chatted over lunch about some friends she'd met by chance in town and about the tax letters from their accountant which had arrived whilst she was out. As Tom made some tea, Liz broached the real subject of the day.

"Let's think about what you're trying to search for, Tom," Liz prompted suddenly, "We know Brophy and you look like twins and you think that American guy or whoever he was in Bonn, mistook you for him. Right?"

"Yep, that's about it," said Tom dryly.

"So, you think, I think, Daan and Boukje think, that there was some sort of message in that briefcase intended for Brophy. Right again?"

"Yep."

"Well, is the fact that you were in Germany of any importance?"

"Not sure," said Tom, becoming a little more interested, "Seemed to me it might be that whatever was being planned was to happen there. Otherwise, why do the thing there at all—and especially in front of all that military and police's presence?"

"Could be that Germany and Bonn was just convenient. Could be the courier, the American, worked there and it was easier for Brophy to go to Germany than for him to travel to Ireland. Did Brophy speak German?"

"No idea," said Tom, feeling both slightly embarrassed that he hadn't thought about such an obvious point, and also increasingly intrigued by Liz's line of questioning.

"If you forget about Germany and concentrate on the deal, maybe you can focus a bit better?" Liz's tone was, as usual, clinical, but also supportive and encouraging.

"I've considered all the information I can find on IRA's plans and deals in the mid-seventies and nothing ever mentions Ger…" Tom stopped, realising what he was doing. Scanning the information, he had focussed on the German link and largely dismissed other information.

"So, the point is, with which of these plans Brophy would be most likely to be involved?" he kind of asked and stated at the same time.

"Could be a good angle," said Liz encouragingly.

"Well, we know he was a suit, not an assassin, skilled at financial wheeler-dealing and probably big-money stuff."

"Why don't you go back through all that information and speculation and draw up a list of anything that might have needed 'big money'," said Liz, "You've got all afternoon until about six."

"Great stuff, Liz, great stuff," said Tom, giving her a big hug. "By the way, what happens at six?"

"Des and Anne, our new neighbours, are coming around. Remember? It was you who made the arrangement," Liz said, trying not to show her exasperation.

It was simple, really. Liz had taken Tom back to some first principles. Whilst he had been preoccupied with the German connection, she had reminded him that it was Brophy's link with a big plan or deal that was the important first connection. If that could be established, the next step was to fill in the details: Germany, the briefcase, the American. Tom went back through his notes.

Remember 'big', Tom said to himself. *Brophy was a big player.*

Tom also recalled Daan's message. Harris had said that Brophy probably failed to deliver on a big plan. No use then, looking at things that actually succeeded. Better to focus on what it was that the Provos were planning but which never happened.

Several stories seemed at first sight to be worth a further look. First, a rumoured link between Gaddafi and the IRA with the former to fund major atrocities in the UK. Second, suggestions of the Provos linking formally with the Basque Separatist movement, the Red Army Faction and other terrorist organisations with funding from a major (unknown) source. Third, a major funding coup in America with an (again) unknown donor prepared to fund 'the final push' by the IRA in Ireland. Then, there was a recurring story: assassination of the Queen and/or Prince Charles, and/or other sovereign heads of state or members of royal families across Europe.

"You've half-an-hour," came the voice from the hallway, echoing up through the house.

"OK," Tom shouted from the study, whilst quietly thinking, *Oh, shit.*

Chapter Ten
November 2001

"Tom will be down in a minute," Liz said, taking Des and Anne's coats.

Des and Anne were both good, fun and seemingly sensible people. Tom emerged into the living room where the gas log-fire was burning brightly and the conversation was even brighter.

"Hi, both," he said, "Good to see you. What about a drink?" Tom poured wine and the conversation resumed.

Anne and Des had recently moved into the seven letting-room guesthouse along the street. It was a life-changing move, a chance to do something completely different. A kind of dream-realisation, like Fairholme was for Liz. The guesthouse was a potential gold mine, but they'd realised quickly that it needed more work on the building than they had anticipated. They were up to their eyes in 'brickies', joiners, plasterers, roofers and decorators, all working to really tight deadlines so that they could meet obligations to bookings made before they became the new owner-occupiers.

The conversation meandered around the basic theme that every time someone did something in the house, they uncovered another problem to be fixed. Tom enjoyed DIY and simple building work and had built-up quite a stock of knowledge over years of renovating places he'd lived in, so this was an interesting distraction. Eventually, though, his mind began to wander back to Brophy. Des was an intelligent and attentive guest.

"So, enough of builder's bums and chimneys that go crash in the night, what's been keeping you so busy, Tom? Haven't seen you for weeks." Liz glanced up briefly from her conversation with Anne which had moved on as well to stuff about other neighbours, of sons, daughters and grandsons.

"Been busy at work, as usual," Tom said, "And working on a sort of personal project in my spare time."

"C'mon," said Liz, "Spill the beans, Tom. You know you're itching to."

Anne and Des knew nothing of Tom's past.

"Why don't we move into the dining room and you can tell them the whole thing over dinner."

"OK."

"Boy, I'm all ears," said Des.

Dinner was one of Liz and Tom's favourite meals. Chicken breast marinated in chilli, lemon juice, garlic and tarragon cooked in a cream sauce with sun-dried tomatoes and chestnut mushrooms, served with broccoli and green French beans.

"This is absolutely delicious," said Anne, "Must take the recipe."

"Certainly, we must," said Des, "But I'll get indigestion soon if you don't get to this tale, Tom."

Tom tried desperately to give them the short version of Bonn and Belfast: of sitting with Boukje and Daan in the Pyrenees, of Declan Brophy and the IRA, but even so the main course, Liz's plum tarte tatin with crème fraiche and coffee all came and went before he'd finished. Of course, and as usual, it wasn't all Tom. Anne and Des interrupted regularly with questions and observations and the odd exclamation of disbelief. Liz added bits of detail here and there which Tom had missed. Tom poured brandy for himself and port for Liz, Anne and Des.

"I still don't really see the link, Tom," said Anne sipping her port.

"Neither do I, Anne," said Tom with a hint of genuine frustration, "But my guts tell me there must be one. It's all too much of a coincidence otherwise and I now don't accept the German police's explanation for me getting dumped with the briefcase."

Des had sat for some time saying nothing, simply playing with his port glass from which he took the occasional sip and staring into the rapidly declining candle at the far end of the table.

"Fancy joining us, Des?" Anne said a touch sardonically, nudging his elbow.

"It *must* be the briefcase," said Des distantly, "If there's a connection, then that must be it."

"Sure, Des," said Tom, perhaps a little sharply for a pleasant conversation with good people, after a superb meal and over some excellent brandy and port.

"A message for Brophy would have been in code," Des continued, as if he hadn't heard Tom at all, "And I know a really good code breaker, don't I, Anne?"

"Well, I like crosswords if that's what you mean," said Anne rather meekly.

"So does Liz," Tom said, "And she's really great at them."

"Maybe," said Liz, pouring the last of the coffee, "But you need a clue to solve and we don't have one. That's what I've been trying to get Tom to find. The clue that might link to the briefcase."

Whether it was Des' oh-so-obvious comment or the effects of the brandy or both (he was never sure on reflection) but suddenly, Tom was overwhelmed by a sense that he was under attack. As if he didn't know that a message would be in code. As if he didn't know you needed a clue to solve a puzzle. As if he hadn't been working into the small hours most nights for weeks to find the link. Typical Tom. When he felt like this, he went onto the attack. Something in his genes or upbringing—or both.

"Well, had you given me time, I'd have told you that I think I've found it," he said assertively but pleasantly, or so he thought. Liz gave him a reproving and sharp glance.

"It's got something to do with killing the Queen." As he said the words, he had no idea why he was saying them. Sure, there had been speculation in the mid-seventies that the IRA was planning something along these lines, but it had lots of other plans too. True to form, though, when in this mood, there was no hint of uncertainly in Tom's voice.

"Good Lord," said Anne and Liz together in a loud and almost falsetto pitch.

"Pen, paper and that list of things in the briefcase," said Des, clearing glasses and table mats to make space. "We're going to crack the code."

"You mean *we're* going to crack the code, I think," said Anne pointing at herself and Liz, "Don't know about Tom, but you're about as much use with crosswords as a chocolate teapot is for making tea."

"About the same, or even less," said Liz, squeezing Tom's hand in a show of support. Tom grunted and shrugged assent. Liz was quite right after all.

Tom got some paper and pens and listed the items: briefcase, book, shoelace, pencil and paper clip. Liz and Anne began to disassemble the words. At the top of the page, they wrote 'Queen', 'Kill' and 'Assassinate' and chatted feverishly about crossword-type traditions and formula. At first, Des and Tom joined in, but after only a few minutes, it became clear to both of them that they were indeed as much use as chocolate teapots.

It was now just passed midnight. Liz, Anne and Des had punters' breakfasts to do that morning. It would be an early start. Nothing seemed to be coming from the increasing pile of scrapped paper.

"The book was by Jules Verne, wasn't it, Tom?" said Liz, "What was it called again?"

"Robur, the Conqueror, is the best translation, I think," said Tom, somewhat sleepily, "Though there have been others. It was actually in German: Robur der Eroberer. Here it is. All I kept of the case and the other stuff," he said, taking the book from the alcove shelves.

Tom and Des retired from the scene of cryptic-clue battling to the living room where Tom filled in more details of Belfast which had intrigued Des.

They chatted about their respective pasts too. The events that had led them to this point.

Tom had been born and raised in the West Midlands, about seven miles from Birmingham, in the so-called Black Country. Legend had it that the name came from a comment by Queen Victoria, as she observed the miles and miles of factories and terraced house chimneys, belching black smoke covering everything with soot, on a train journey north from London. Tom could recall something of that landscape, though, even in his childhood and adolescence, in the '60s, it had already begun to decline as the manufacturing powerhouse of the country. Huge factories were being replaced by shopping centres, new roads and housing estates, or just demolished and left as wasteland. He had mixed emotions about his roots.

On the one hand, he cringed when he heard his native accent on TV and when he visited his hometown to see his folks. He found the place depressingly dark and gloomy. The people always seemed to be trying desperately to look fashionable but largely failing. It seemed as if every kid had to yell at the top of their voice and every parent had to drag them around and yell back at them in an even louder voice. The shop 'where everything is a £1' was always crowded and so was the street market. And for every young mum or young person, there seemed to be at least nine who were old. Of these, every other one looked frail in poor health, limping, shuffling, walking very slowly, looking into shops but rarely going in. Being the powerhouse of manufacturing had taken a heavy toll.

"On the other hand," Tom said, "I don't want to and can't anyway, forget my past. I had some great times. Forged really significant and lasting friendships during those seventeen years before I went to university. And, I find it hard to beat the humour, the banter, the 'crack', as they call it down there. I knew some remarkable people too. My two best mates' parents, for example. Stoic, strong people who faced really hard times—and not just financially—with a quiet spirit, a determination and always a joke or a funny side. They are all 'can-do' people and if I have inherited anything worthwhile from that culture, then I hope that is it." Tom took a good slug of brandy. He'd probably not said these things to more than a handful of people before. Maybe to no one, not even Liz.

"Think I know at least a bit of what you mean," said Des. "On the plus side, Leeds left me with two indelible marks: a passion for Rugby League and a desire to be friends with everyone. One problem is that neither of these two attributes gets you anywhere in Kent where I washed-up after working in a few other places. Also, on the downside, Anne tells me—and I know she's right, but I won't admit it—I've got a bloody-minded 'I'm right', Yorkshire streak. I also hate people telling me they know what it's like 'in places like Leeds when they haven't been further north than Luton and it's always said in a patronising sort of 'sorry old chap' kind-of way." Des finished his glass, nipped next door to the dining room and returned with a fully refreshed one.

"Mind you," he continued as if there had been no break in his flow, "I've mellowed a lot since I met Anne." Tom finished his brandy and poured another.

"A bit of a tyke, as they say in Yorkshire. Jack-the-lad, into this and that. My auntie, May, called me a rebel. My uncle, Joe, preferred hooligan. Reckon my auntie was right. Always have had that streak in me. Helped me no end when I got into sales and helped me meet Anne. Whisked her from under the nose of a filthy rich type at a dance by pretending I was her minder hired by her dad—a city tycoon, I said—to look after her. Anyway, the move here has been the best thing we could have ever done—providing the bloody place doesn't fall down before we've paid off the mortgage!"

Tom realised there were more tales to share with Des. Like the time in Amsterdam when Tom all but destroyed a bedroom doorframe and part of the door in a small hotel because the plastic key had broken and he was determined Liz wouldn't sleep on the landing all night. But that one would keep. He was too tired now.

It was now nearly 02:00 and Tom was feeling pretty guilty. For one thing, he had no real idea that 'Killing the Queen' had anything to do with all this. For another, he could sleep in a little as his first meeting wasn't until 11.00, but Liz had to be on the breakfast trail by 07.30 and Anne and Des too. Saying that they should call it a night might seem as if he wanted their guests to go, irrespective of anything, which wasn't true. However, say nothing and by the sounds from the dining room, they'd all still be at it come dawn.

"That's it! That's it! It must be! God, do you think it is, was, er...Tom, Des!" Liz called. Tom heard the shouting from the dining room first and shot out of the settee as if he'd been bitten on the backside by a scorpion. Des was just a nano-second behind him.

"Not so loud, Liz. Remember the punters upstairs, eh?" Liz looked suitably admonished, but nothing could dampen her enthusiasm just now.

"We've got it. Well, at least we've got something," she said, her voice trembling with excitement. She was standing; Anne still seated beside her, facing a table strewn with bits of paper surrounding a virtually empty bottle of port. They both looked knackered but also, curiously, wide awake.

"Look!" said Liz, spreading out a sheet of A4 before them. "It's in the title of the book. The German title."

Tom and Des saw before them the title of the book written:

*R*OB*U*R D*E*R ER*O*BERER
Underneath were the following words:
D BRO U ROB 4(x) ER
Des broke the silence.

"Declan Brophy to rob four 'ER's'," he shouted.

"What the hell are ER's?" asked Tom.

"Elizabeth Regina, The Queen, you bozo," said Liz in a friendly, if somewhat exasperated and definitely disbelieving tone.

"Four?" asked Des and Tom almost together.

"Well, maybe it means four Queens in Europe," said Anne.

"Or, maybe four members of the Royal Family here or somewhere else," said Liz.

"Bloody hell," said Tom, "I need a cigarette and a coffee."

Chapter Eleven
November 2001

"Perhaps, Dr Cooper has a view?" Tom heard the words only just in time and had no idea on what he might have a view. It was almost 12.30. The meeting was already well over an hour old and proving to be one of the more uninspiring quality and standards committee meetings. Tom had overall responsibility for curriculum strategy in the university. It was a senior position and one he enjoyed.

Thinking about how university courses would need to look in the early part of the twenty-first century, what the market for university education would demand in the next few years and trying to position the university to meet these were all stimulating challenges. However, today, after a really late but exciting night, he had other enthralling matters on his mind. Experienced meetings-person that he was, he made several assertive but noncommittal responses having glanced first at the agenda and guessing rightly the item they were discussing. The chair of the committee seemed not only satisfied, but almost impressed. Several committee members nodded sagely. Everyone seemed content.

"You're away with the fairies, Tom, if you think we're going down that road," said Jane, Tom's normally trustworthy ally in the University Executive Group as they walked together across the campus and, in Tom's case, to another meeting.

"Most people seemed to think it was at least a good starting point," Tom said adroitly.

"Maybe, but where the hell did you get that idea in the first place? First time I or anyone else has heard of it. Didn't think to share this hair-brained scheme beforehand?" Jane was miffed.

"No damage done, Jane," Tom said steadfastly, as he tripped briefly on a kerbstone.

"Next time, you'll land flat on your face and deserve it," Jane chuckled, feeling the gods must be on her side.

It had been a long and tiring day but 'the five queens' hadn't left Tom for long at any time. He couldn't wait to get home, see Liz and move everything forward. He'd had so many new thoughts and ideas.

It was after seven pm when he arrived home—a typical day in that respect. Liz was on the phone taking another booking. Tom uncorked a bottle of South African Shiraz, poured Liz a Pinot Grigio from the fridge and examined his post. A typical day's haul. A bill from the cable telephone and television supplier, a catalogue advertising every DIY gadget known to humankind, a letter telling him again that he should replace their current car with a new one at a knockdown price reserved only for him as a 'specially valued customer' and his favourite—another letter from somewhere in the States, explaining that he had already won $200,000 via a random postcode draw and all he need do is register his claim. He couldn't be sure, but it seemed these lottery letters had increased in frequency since the launch of the guesthouse website.

"Hello, my darling," Liz said as she came off the telephone. "It's been hectic here all day. That was the fifth booking I've taken today and we've got two Australians in tonight who just knocked on the front door this morning. Strange looking couple. He's about seven feet tall and she's about five feet high and eight feet round. They want two full-English breakfasts. I think he'll have some grapefruit segments and she'll have the rest!" Liz laughed out loud.

Such observations between them about 'the punters' were not unusual. Tom mentally recalled a conversation about a young couple who turned out to be even more interesting than they looked. He was tall, with long frizzy hair, reminiscent of the styles of rock band guitarists and lead singers in the seventies. She was five feet five, or so, with a mane of very red hair. Both were striking in different ways, but also because they were dressed entirely in black. They were quiet and pleasant but on their second day, a Sunday, Liz discovered some 'odd' stuff.

"When I went into the bedroom to service it, there it was, in all its glory. Laid out on the bed was a…well…a…sort of a…meringue dress. Perfectly laid out, just as you might wear it. Alongside it was this huge sword. I mean, the bed is a super king-size and this sword stretched from top to toe. Well, almost. It looked sort of ceremonial. Then, when they came down to breakfast, she was wearing a T-shirt which said 'Obey' across the chest with a sword drawn vertically through the word."

What had transpired in the bedroom the previous night probably didn't bear thinking about—but they speculated anyway! It was Liz who broke the bawdy conversation.

"Anyway, enough of punters and my day, what kind of day has my sweetheart sleuth had?"

Tom physically winced at the idea he was a sleuth and Liz had a cheeky laugh-out-loud at his reaction. He began with a very brief run through his diary, people he'd seen and some gossip about the Vice-Chancellor he'd picked up from a good 'confident' at a regional meeting of university executive leads for curriculum development. Not that juicy, but it had livened up an otherwise pretty routine, if tiring, day.

"So," said Liz, "Had any thoughts about Brophy?"

"Sure have," Tom said, pouring another glass of Shiraz and topping up Liz's glass. "I see it this way, the—"

Tom was cut short mid-sentence by the telephone. They both laughed as Liz got up to answer it. This was more than an occasional occurrence. Call it coincidence, but almost every time they started to have a particularly interesting or important conversation during their early evening 'catch-up' each day, the phone was sure to ring. It was most often a booking enquiry, but this time it was Margaret, Liz's friend of several years and about whom Liz had been concerned for some time. As she chatted, Liz looked every few minutes at

Tom, shrugging her shoulders and mouthing, "Sorry, but what can I do?" Tom mouthed 'no problem' in return, raising his right thumb in the air and disappeared upstairs to change out of his 'uniform'—the dark suit, dark shirt and matching dark tie that had become something of his trademark at the university.

In his usual evening wear of track-suit bottoms, polo shirt and trainers, Tom decided to check his personal email. Liz and Margaret could be chatting a while. Most of Tom's email correspondence was via his university address which he cleared as far as possible at the end of each day. So, he was surprised to see two new one's in the inbox given he'd not long left work. He was even more surprised that one was from Daan (who hadn't emailed for months) and one from Jack in Belfast—who hadn't emailed for a year, at least. However, it was absolutely no coincidence that they had emailed him almost simultaneously that day. Tom read Daan's mail out loud:

"Tom. Heard on the wire that the UK police are opening an investigation into Brophy's activities in the seventies. New information it seems, about a conspiracy. Will get more and be in touch. Say hello to Liz from Boukje and me. Best, Daan."

"Christ Almighty!" Tom exclaimed out loud to himself. As an atheist, he regularly blasphemed, as his grandmother would have called it. Jack's email was even more astonishing. Even the Belfast accent came through.

"Hello, Tom, me old mate. Long-time no hear and all that stuff. Anyway, thought you would want to know that the Garda and the Ulster Constabulary have reopened an old enquiry into plans by the IRA to assassinate Prince Charles. Some new information has been found, Brophy is mentioned twice in the report. Get back to you if I get any more. Give us a call? Myra sends her best to you and Liz, as do I. Keep taking the medicine. Jack."

"Holy Moses," Tom shouted out loud. He sat and stared at the screen, reread each email at least three times and decided to print them to show Liz. Their cheap and overworked printer clunked, whirred and clanked, preparing to print. He could have written them out by hand more quickly, Tom thought in growing frustration.

He burst into the breakfast room clutching the emails. Liz was still on the phone. She raised one finger. A signal that she'd nearly finished.

"Read these!" he shouted, as Liz came off the phone. Tom waited for the reaction.

"Good God!" said Liz sitting down slowly. "What are you going to do, Tom?"

"Well, I'm going to…well, first, I guess I ought to…" he stumbled because he hadn't thought at all about what he would do. "What do you think?"

"First, try and get any more information you can. Second, you have to contact the police, or MI5, or whoever might be in charge over here." Liz's normal, steady and calm voice was now a little shaky.

"And what would I tell them?" Tom said somewhat sarcastically. "I've…you've…solved a pretend puzzle and made two plus two equal four, connecting me to a bizarre coincidence twenty-five years ago that might have something or nothing to do with their enquiries."

"Well, I wouldn't put it quite like that," Liz said with a subtle but clearly discernible exasperation with Tom's attitude. "But the gist of it is exactly what you would say."

"But I'd look such a prat—" Tom suggested, only to be cut short by Liz's clear irritation.

"Oh, for God's sake! They've reopened enquiries about plans to assassinate Charlie-boy and they've figured Brophy has some part in it, somewhere, somehow. Forget the puzzle if you want to. The fact you look like his twin and had some bizarre experiences at that time ought to be enough to interest anyone and certainly them. C'mon Tom."

"I'll call Jack."

"Well, goodness me, it's the lad himself. Thought that email would get you out of your pit." *A typical Jack-welcome,* thought Tom.

"How's Myra? The wee one too?" Tom enquired. They had had a boy, Ben, since Tom had last seen them.

"They're fine. Just dandy. How's the good wife?"

"Thinks I should go to the police with my tales of coincidence. She's fine."

"I was talking with Myra about that just an hour ago, Tom, as it happens. We agree with Liz, even though there's no evidence of any link with plans to bump-off the Prince—"

"But there is, well…sort of…" Tom interjected. He told Jack of the events of the previous Friday with Des and Anne.

"Jesus Christ!" said Jack. "Hey, Myra, they've found a code in the book title and it's about royalty." Tom could just hear in the background a somewhat strangled and muffled 'oh my God'.

"Myra is having a bite before she goes out to a 'leaving do' with folks from work; otherwise known as right royal booze-up," said Jack laughing to himself about that description, given the circumstances.

"Jack, have you got any more info apart from what you said in the email?"

"Not much. Seems, though, that the Garda have been grilling an informant about a load of stuff and he's spilled the beans about these plans in the seventies. He's possibly Dutch, according to the reports. Does that help?"

Tom tossed and turned almost all that night. Sure, he wanted to help the police enquiries. Even more, he wanted to know just how all these events fitted together. But the feeling in the pit of his stomach wouldn't go away. It was fear. What if his name found its way into the press? What if the IRA decided to 'sort him'? They might even attack Liz or someone else in the family. He went round and round all these and other possibilities including, still, the one about looking a complete prat.

Chapter Twelve
November 2001

"Hello, Detective Sergeant Jackson here. I understand you have some information you think might help us? First, may I have your name?"

"Dr Tom Cooper."

"Address? And if you don't mind, your nationality? Thanks. Now tell me, what you have that might be of use to us, Dr Cooper."

"Well, it's a bit complicated. I suppose the easiest thing is that it relates to Declan Brophy and allegations about his involvement in a plot to assassinate Prince Charles which the press says you're investigating."

"And?" said the polite-but-blunt voice at the other end of the telephone.

"Well, Brophy and I look very alike. I think I was mistaken for him twice, once in the seventies, in Germany, and once by the army in Belfast, in the '80s."

"Fascinating, Dr Cooper. And what has any of that to do with us now?"

Sergeant Jackson was clearly not impressed.

"The incident in Germany, in Bonn to be precise, involved my being left with a briefcase by a complete stranger. The police there had no real explanation for it. I think it was meant for Brophy and contained information relating to the Prince Charles' plot." Tom's fear of being thought a real prat was right in front of him. There was no reaction from the other end of the phone. Tom's anxiety heightened.

"Look," he said as firmly as he could muster, "The press say you have information from a Dutchman. I think the guy who gave me the briefcase was Dutch."

"When exactly was this, Dr Cooper?"

"1976."

"It could be helpful if a colleague and I could talk with you face-to-face, Dr Cooper. Could we visit you?"

"Yes, of course. But I will need time from work. When will you come?"

"Let us agree a date now," said Jackson. They appeared on Tom's doorstep almost exactly 24 hours later.

"I am Detective Sergeant Jackson, Dr Cooper, we spoke on the phone yesterday. And this is Commander Fitzsimmons." Both men flashed Metropolitan Police ID cards in Tom's face. "May we come in?"

Jackson was probably about thirty-five, roughly Tom's height and wearing a pretty smart and expensive-looking suit. Fitzsimmons looked to be in his mid-to-late forties, was at least six feet, wore an even smarter—and even more expensive-looking—suit and had a fine tan to boot.

"This is my wife, Liz," Tom said, as he ushered the visitors into the living room.

"Pleased to meet you," said Liz, shaking their hands. "Would you like some tea or coffee?"

"Nothing for us," said Fitzsimmons before Jackson had a chance to reply, "But thank you, anyway."

"We'll get straight down to business if you don't mind, Dr Cooper," Jackson said, opening a small briefcase and extracting two folders. "We've checked your story with the Bonn Police and their records show you were interviewed by them and they inspected a briefcase as you said. You gave a description of the man who left the briefcase with you. More of that in a moment." Jackson opened one of the files, "We'd like to find out about the other incident you mentioned, in Belfast." Tom went through the story and as far as he could tell the same as he'd recounted it (now several times) before. Fitzsimmons and Jackson listened impassively.

"Your friend's name in Belfast? And address?" Jackson asked. Tom hesitated for a moment. "A problem, Dr Cooper?" asked Fitzsimmons assertively.

"Well, er, no. I suppose not," said Tom, "Just that, I haven't told them I'm talking with you about all this. Do they have to get dragged into it?"

"Dr Cooper," Fitzsimmons moved slightly in his chair, looked directly at Liz and spoke as if only to her amidst an audience of several hundred. "For all I know, at this moment, you are one of the IRA's diversionary tacticians or stooges. Someone set up with a plausible story to divert me from the real evidence. And when it's about something that may have involved a threat to the Royal Household, I'll involve anyone, and I mean *anyone*, that I judge should be involved. Your friend's name and address, please?"

Tom, firmly put in his place, duly obliged.

"And what exactly were you asked by the Army Sergeant?" Jackson asked.

"I've already told you as much as I remember," Tom replied, still irritated by the lesson in *'real politik'* from Fitzsimmons.

"I hope you haven't, Dr Cooper, or I may be about to arrest you for wasting police time, at the very least." Fitzsimmons's gaze was steady.

"I can't think of anything I've missed," Tom said, his voice trembling. He glanced at Liz who looked as petrified as he felt.

"If I said that you gave the sergeant a wrong address, Dr Cooper, what would you say?"

"You'd be wrong," Tom said assertively. "I gave him my address and after checking with the soldier in the Land Rover, he asked me if I'd ever had another address in Lancaster. I told him I had and gave him that address too. He seemed satisfied enough."

"Good. We'll be on our way, Dr Cooper. Sergeant Jackson will be contacting you again in a few days. We'll be wanting you to come to London." They both got up and went to the front door. No handshakes, just, "Goodbye, Mrs Cooper," and they were gone.

"I need a drink."

"Me too."

Chapter Thirteen
December 2001

The days had come and gone with no contact from Jackson. Tom had called Jack on the evening of the visit. Jack was fine about Tom giving the police his address.

"Hey man, no problem at all. I'll just have to hide the contraband, drugs and porno videos a bit better, that's all," he chortled, laughing at his own joke in that infectious way he had.

Over the days, Tom and Liz got on with life but spoke a lot of the visit from 'J and F', as they had come to refer to them. Two things dominated their conversations. To begin with, Tom repeatedly questioned why they had not returned to the topic of the Dutchman and what happened in Bonn, as Jackson had implied they would. He and Liz agreed that this would be the main point of the visit to London. This made sense because it was clear that the only real purpose of the visit to their home had been to check Tom out—'eyeball him', as the phrase goes. Their second main topic of conversation was Fitzsimmons' quiz about Belfast.

"They know all about Belfast, Tom," said Liz. "They were just checking that you knew what they knew about it."

"And giving me a fright too was part of the plan," said Tom, briefly re-living the sense of panic. "They were letting me know, in no uncertain terms, that this is a serious business." It was ten days since the visit to Fairholme by J and F when Tom took the call at work.

"Dr Cooper here."

"Sergeant Jackson, Dr Cooper. Are you able to talk at the moment?"

"Yes, I'm on my own in my office."

"Good. Commander Fitzsimmons asks you to be at Paddington Green Police Station tomorrow at 11.00 am. Will you have any problem with that?"

"Well, I've three pretty important meetings tomorrow which I cannot really reschedule. The day after tomorrow would be much easier."

"We'll expect you at 11.00 am tomorrow then."

"But… I've just said that—"

"See you tomorrow, Dr Cooper." *Click*, and the phone went dead.

Tom spent the next hour rearranging two meetings—and taking the moans and groans on the chin for his pains—and cajoling Jane to chair the other meeting in his absence.

"It's a personal matter, Jane. Rather not go into detail, but if you could step in… I know it's really very short notice but… Jane, you know, you're a genuine star."

That evening, Tom and Liz rehearsed the Bonn and Belfast tales until they were almost exhausted. They collapsed into bed pretty early, knowing they both had early starts.

Liz came back into the breakfast room, having deposited full breakfasts in front of two boisterous young Welsh women in the dining room.

"Time I was gone," Tom said, checking he had his tickets.

"Just tell them everything you know, Tom, I'll be just there." Liz pointed at his right shoulder and gave him a big hug, "Call me on your way back?"

Tom tried to do some paperwork on the train and managed to write a couple of letters and some notes to himself of jobs he must do when he got back to the university. For the most part though, he just sat and looked out of the window, trying to recall everything about Bonn.

"Just take a seat, sir," said the Desk Sergeant who looked about sixteen, but was probably in his late thirties. Paddington Green was the top-security police station in London at the time. Renowned for hosting gangland criminals and terrorists, it looked like something out of the films *1984* or *Metropolis*. It also reminded him of the police station he'd passed in

Belfast all those years ago. *No better stimulus for remembering those days,* he thought to himself as he went to the security gate.

"Dr Tom Cooper to see Commander Fitzsimmons."

Eventually it was Jackson, not Fitzsimmons, who appeared and led Tom through several doors, down three corridors and into a small room. Even if the pit in his stomach led him to the incredibly stupid idea of running for it, he wouldn't have had a clue which way to go.

"Hello again, Dr Cooper. Thank you for making the journey." Fitzsimmons sat behind a small table. Tom suddenly had a sense of déjà-vu. The language was different but, for all the world, this was just like the situation in the police station that night in Bonn. From memory, even the colour of the walls was the same. Tom was ushered to a chair on the opposite side of the table from Fitzsimmons. Jackson sat on a chair with a notepad on his knee, a little distance away. Déjà-vu again.

"You are right, Dr Cooper. You and Brophy do look alike." Fitzsimmons handed Tom a picture, "Perhaps, not quite as much now as then. The gods appear to have been a tad kinder to our Mr Brophy in the hair department over the years." Fitzsimmons smiled and glanced at Jackson. Tom said nothing. Fitzsimmons was right.

"So, tell me, what made you think the briefcase was meant for Brophy all those years ago in Germany?"

Tom went through his own trains of thought, his eventual dissatisfaction with the police explanation; the realisation after recounting both, the Belfast and Bonn incidents to Boukje and Daan, that Brophy might be a link: how the suspicion grew once he found out more about Brophy's past and most recently, the press reports about the Prince Charles plot in the seventies.

"Yet, the Bonn police found nothing suspicious in the briefcase," Jackson stated coldly.

"No, but we think we know what was in it," Tom said quickly and for the first time, confidently.

"We're all ears," Jackson said without looking up from his notepad.

Tom recounted the story of how Liz decoded the title of the book. He deliberately left out the part played by Anne wanting desperately to keep as many friends out of this as possible. Without a flicker of interest in any of that, Fitzsimmons asked Tom where the briefcase and its contents were then.

"Last I knew, they were with the woman I lived with, in Germany. I left in late 1977 and I haven't seen her or the briefcase since. I have the book though."

"We'll need to see it, Dr Cooper." Tom suddenly felt a surge of true delight welling-up inside him.

"You didn't ask about it when you came a week ago and you didn't ask me to bring it."

"We'll make arrangements for you to deposit it at your local nick," Jackson said.

"No need. I have it here. Seemed obvious to me you would want to see it." Tom was triumphant. "Yes!" he said quietly to himself, taking the small brown book from his briefcase and placing it in front of Fitzsimmons. Fitzsimmons handed the book immediately to Jackson without so much as a glance at it and continued, as if none of the last five minutes had happened. He moved a file that had been sitting unopened to his left into the middle of the table.

"I have some pictures here, about thirty, which I'd like you to look at, Dr Cooper. I realise it's over 25 years ago and it might be difficult, but we'd like to see if anyone in this gallery of the bad and the very bad reminds you of the man who gave you the briefcase." Fitzsimmons' tone was somehow less abrasive. He opened the file, turned it through 180°, and slid it in front of Tom.

"Take your time. You'd like a tea or coffee, I expect?"

"Er, well, yes. Tea, with milk and one sugar would be great," Tom said in amazement. The first sign that J and F were actually warm-blooded creatures was a shock. Jackson got up and left the room. Fitzsimmons moved to the small, fairly high window and with his back to Tom, stood motionless, gazing at whatever was to be seen outside.

Tom looked at the first page. It was blank. He turned it over to reveal ten passport-sized 'mugshots'. Some had printed numbers and letters across the bottom—criminal record numbers—but some didn't.

It had always been amazing to Tom that even on the day he had sat and chatted to the guy for possibly half-an-hour overlooking the Rhine, he couldn't give a very good description of him to the police. In the years between, he had often tried to recall more detail, but nothing had really come to mind. He didn't even have a clear image of the man's face. The only hope was that one of these pictures would spark a memory. He studied each picture carefully. Nothing. He turned to the next page. Immediately his gaze was drawn to the picture in the bottom left-hand corner. He was almost about to shout out "That's him! That's him!" when the door opened and in walked Jackson with two cups of tea.

"Milk and sugar as you said, Dr Cooper."

"Er, yes, thanks," said Tom. He sipped at the strongest cup of tea he'd ever tasted and stared at the picture. Was it? Wasn't it? Could be. Was he sure? He decided to turn the page. *Look at them all first,* he said to himself. He wished he hadn't.

"Well, Dr Cooper? Any thoughts?" Fitzsimmons returned to the table.

"I think it could be this one," Tom said, pointing to the picture bottom-left on the second page. He felt sick and thought he might actually throw up. He sipped his tea and gulped in air.

"Interesting," Fitzsimmons said flatly. "It's our man, Jackson," he said. Tom looked at Jackson, who scribbled on his note pad and smiled to himself.

"Most helpful, Dr Cooper. I think that's all for today. We'll return the book at some point. Jackson, will give you a receipt before you leave. By the way, are you feeling OK? You look rather pale."

"I'm fine," Tom lied, "To be honest, I think the tea has—
"

"A bit strong perhaps," Fitzsimmons said laughing. Tom nodded weakly. "Oh, and just one other thing before you go. Surprised you didn't mention the photo on the last page." Tom looked up and stared at Fitzsimmons like a rabbit caught in headlights on a dark country lane.

Chapter Fourteen
December 2001

"Hello, my darling. Yes, I'm fine." Tom did his best to sound OK, "I'm on the train, should be home in a couple of hours. Yes, I'll tell you all about it then—we keep going through tunnels and I lose the signal. Yes, sure, I'm OK. Fill you in later. Love you loads too."

Tom opened a can of lager and stared across the fields of East Anglia, kissed by the early evening sun, speeding by. After leaving Paddington Green, he'd wandered around for a while, largely unaware of his surroundings or where he walked, focussed only on that picture on the last page of Fitzsimmons' file. Eventually, he decided to get a taxi to Kings' Cross, being too tired to think about the Underground. He was confused and knackered. Nothing made sense.

He got off the train, fought his way weakly through the hordes of people returning home from work or wherever they had been, walked from the station on autopilot and eventually turned the corner into his own street and prepared, as best he could, to try and explain things to Liz.

"So glad you're home," Liz said, giving him a tight and lingering hug. "I've a glass of red on the table. You look like you need it." They sat at the breakfast table. Tom sipped his wine.

"So?" Liz said gently, but with a hint of desperation for the news.

Tom ran though the day's events. It seemed he'd identified their Dutch informant as the guy in Bonn. They'd kept the book, presumably for tests, and seemed not that interested in the decoding of its title, but then they didn't give much away at all.

"And after all that bloody hard work by Anne and me too," Liz said in a genuinely deflated, disappointed, not to say angry, tone. "So, will you have to see J and F again?" Tom had thought a lot about this on the journey home.

"They didn't say they wanted to see me again, but I must see them I think, Liz." Tom took another slug of wine. Liz looked perplexed but before she could ask him, Tom got to the main point.

"You see, when I was looking at the mugshots, there was someone else there that I knew apart from the—"

"Someone else?" Liz's voice was at least an octave higher than normal. There was a pause before she said, "Ah. Brophy, I suppose."

"No, it was Monika."

"Monika? Monika who?" Liz was genuinely bemused.

"How many Monika's have I known?" said Tom, pouring more wine.

"You mean Monika who you lived with in Germany? I mean, what the...how the... Good God!" Liz went to the fridge and poured herself a wine.

"I've no idea." Tom looked at her with a disbelieving stare, "I mean, who'd have thought it. It wasn't a bunch of photos of everyone I've ever known. It was, I assume, people the anti-terrorist squad have something on, you know, suspects or informants or such like."

"Are you sure it was her?" Liz leaned backwards on her chair and continued to look bemused. "It was a long time ago, Tom."

"Liz, I'm more sure it was Monika than I am that the Dutchman I fingered was actually the guy in Bonn."

"And what did J and F say exactly?"

"Fitzsimmons said he was surprised I hadn't mentioned the photo on the last page. That was the one of Monika. It must have been. I didn't recognise any others." Tom drained his glass, "I'm going to change, Liz. And tomorrow, I'm calling Jackson."

Chapter Fifteen
A week before Christmas 2001

"Ah, Dr Cooper. We thought we might be hearing from you again." Jackson's voice had 'smug' running all through it.

"You knew that I knew Monika von Strauss in Germany, didn't you? That was her photo in the file. The one Commander Fitzsimmons referred to." Tom was nervous but determined to be assertive.

"We did, Dr Cooper, and you no doubt would like to know what her photo was doing in our files?"

"Of course." Tom was not going to let Jackson off the phone until he knew.

"This isn't a conversation for the telephone, Dr Cooper. There is quite a lot to explain and Commander Fitzsimmons will want to do that. Can you get to London again tomorrow?"

"No," Tom was defiant, "And in any case, I want to know *now*. You owe me that."

"Actually, Dr Cooper, we owe you nothing. However, the Commander is to be in Leeds the day after tomorrow. He can meet you at the rail station, in the bar just inside the side entrance, around 5.00 pm. Do you know the one?"

"Yes."

"And would *that* be convenient?" It would have been possible to cut the irritation in Jackson's voice with a knife.

"Well, er, yes. I guess so. I'll be there."

Tom called Liz from his office. Not at home. *Of course,* Tom said to himself, looking at the digital clock at the bottom right-hand corner of his PC screen, 'lunch with "the girls"'. This was a weekly get-together in Liz's diary. Tom had never met Laura and Jenny, but they were apparently good company and there was always some gossip to report from the 'B&B mafia'. Tom emailed instead.

"Jackson gave nothing away. The bugger. However, meeting Fitzsimmons in Leeds the day after tomorrow to get the story. Love you loads 'n loads 'n loads, xxxxx."

The rest of the day and the next passed Tom by—like so many had in recent weeks. Sure, he turned up at meetings, replied to a mass of emails, dealt with post, talked formally and chatted informally with various colleagues. To all who didn't know, Tom was his usual 'can-do', enthusiastic and proactive self. Liz knew better. For two days, they didn't talk about the meeting coming-up with Fitzsimmons in Leeds. In fact, they talked about anything and everything but Leeds, yet she knew that Tom was really sitting in the bar in the Rail Station already.

Tom left the university in plenty of time. He gave his outward ticket to the clearly bored, impassive guard at the platform automatic exit-barrier at Leeds—which wasn't working again—and headed for the bar just inside the side entrance to the station, near the taxi-rank and bus stops. The bar wasn't as busy as he had seen it before. He scanned the room. Usual mixture of folk but no Fitzsimmons. Tom ordered a Stella and chose a table near the main door. It was 4.30 pm.

Five o'clock came and went, as did 5.15 pm. Tom was getting increasingly frustrated.

"Sorry to be a little late. The meeting dragged on a bit," Fitzsimmons said, as he stood over Tom. "Let me get you a top up? Stella?"

"Thanks." Tom wondered briefly how Fitzsimmons knew he would have Stella, thinking the policeman's knack for summing up people was quite remarkable, until he handed him his glass and noticed Stella Artois engraved on two sides.

"Look," Tom said, leaning forward in his chair, arms spread out across the table, "How come Monika von Strauss' picture was in your file?"

"She is known to us, Dr Cooper."

"Call me Tom. No one—well, hardly anyone—calls me Dr Cooper."

"Fine, Tom," Fitzsimmons said, without any hint that he might reciprocate the offer.

"I guessed that but why and—"

"Tom, listen. I must be on a train out of here at 6.18 pm. We've barely forty-five minutes. Best, I think, that I give you the full story?" Tom nodded and took a gulp of Stella.

"We first got to know von Strauss in the very early '70s. Nothing much, just some suspicions about her friends. Her very regular visits to the UK also seemed interesting, despite her being a teacher of English. When our Dutch 'friend' began to squeal, he mentioned lots of people on our files including von Strauss. Again, nothing very certain. Then he told us of a job he'd done in Bonn, in 1976. Acted as a courier. Unknown recipient and he had no details of what he was handing over, only that it was 'a big job'. He mentioned your friend, Brophy."

"Not my friend," Tom said swiftly, eyes on stalks.

"Whatever, Tom. Once he mentioned him, this made the whole thing much more interesting. We knew Brophy was very well-connected—not only to the Provos, but to the Red Army and other terrorist groups. He was very well-known among crooked, big financiers and especially those trading arms."

"I knew it," Tom said eagerly.

"Knew what?"

"The briefcase was for Brophy via our Dutchman—"

"He's called van Voet," Fitzsimmons interjected.

"Van Voet... Mistook me for him."

"'fraid not, Tom." Fitzsimmons sipped his white wine, "You were the intended courier, Tom. The briefcase had to get to von Strauss."

Tom sat back in his chair, glass in hand, held midway between the table and his mouth opened.

"But you mean? I mean…"

"Yes." Fitzsimmons lent forward across the table, "Perfect for them, Tom. You were a complete innocent. They gambled you'd take the briefcase to the police. The local police had no reason to look too closely, why should they? They did a decent job—took prints, etc. None of them matched any villains known to them and they didn't check with us or Interpol. Even if they had, at that time, we didn't have van Voet on our files, nor did Interpol."

Tom was struggling to take it all in. His mind was racing.

"But Belfast?" he said suddenly, "The link with Brophy."

"No link, Tom." Fitzsimmons finished his wine and glanced at his watch. "By the early '90s, you had been on our files for over five years. If I had shown the rogues' gallery I showed to you last week to someone in 1985 or thereabouts, you'd have been there. No, the Army and the RUC were interested in you, Tom."

"But…what the hell had I… I mean, for God's sake, I wasn't a terrorist or whatever. What the…" Tom was, for once in his life, genuinely speechless.

"You'd acted as a courier for the Provos. And besides, you had a background."

"Background?" Tom shouted, so a couple on the next table jumped. He was apoplectic and now getting really angry.

"Mid-eighties. Who was it who hosted a visit by an active member of the African National Congress to the UK to talk to the local Labour Party in Hertfordshire? Who was it who said at that meeting that from the comfort of England, it was easy to say violence was never justified in political struggles, but it would be different if 'we' were in Cape Town or the Bantustans? Think about it, Tom. If you had been putting that together with Bonn, what would you have thought?"

"But, well, I've never done anything like that. I mean, well… Holy Jesus." Tom drained his glass and sat back in his chair.

"I have to go." Fitzsimmons stood up. Tom did likewise.

"You won't be required any further, Tom. Don't ask me anymore. For one thing, I have no time and for another, I can't tell you, anyway."

Fitzsimmons held out his hand and Tom shook it. He probably should have said all sorts of things, but he couldn't find any words.

Chapter Sixteen
March 2002

The doctor finished his rounds and walked with the policeman down the corridor, away from the ICU and the small wards nearby, to his office. He started to make some notes in the file that sat on his desk.

Detective Inspector Charlie Williams (or 'Barnsley Charlie' as he was known back at The Yard and who had been assigned to this case) sat down opposite.

"What's the prognosis then, Doctor?"

"Well, despite the very best efforts of the maniac driving that car or whatever it was, he's going to live. Remember, though, he has two broken legs, one with multiple fractures, three broken ribs, a broken collarbone and a shattered elbow, and a good number of cuts and bruises. Apart from that catalogue of minor injuries," he glanced at the policeman with a knowing sort of look, "He has suffered severe concussion, acute shock and trauma. Thanks to some great work by the nurses and trauma specialists here, he's able to take a few faltering steps using sticks and additional help. Even so, his physical recovery will take a very long time and a lot of further care."

"All that said, I think we will be sending him home in the next few days if he continues to make the progress he's made so far—tough as they come, this one. We need every bed we have these days. He has a wife at home who can look after him. She's been here every day since he was admitted…er…that was… Let's see…er…over a month ago," he said, flicking to the admission pages of Tom's casefile.

"She seems very caring, so I think he'll be in good hands. He'll also get physio every few days and probably for many weeks. He may need counselling but that decision will be made by others and can wait for now anyway. And he'll have to attend Outpatients here or his local hospital, probably every week for the first few weeks at least."

"What about his memory?"

"Well, that's anybody's guess," he said with a wry smile, as he realised his choice of words. "It could come back fully one day without any advance indication. On the other hand, it might come back in dribs-and-drabs over several weeks or months, but never fully recover. It may not come back at all."

"And the woman injured at the same time?" Barnsley Charlie shuffled in his seat. He'd been seated for far too long today and his arthritis was telling him so.

"She's been discharged already, I believe. However, she's been under another doctor so you will have to check about that."

"Thank you, Doctor."

DI Williams walked back down the corridor towards Tom's small, single room. Liz was sitting outside. She cut a lonely and forlorn figure that sat alone on a single hospital chair in an otherwise empty and large corridor, whilst Tom was having some dressings changed. She was bent very slightly forward, hands clasped together resting in her lap, whilst staring motionless at the floor. She simply couldn't stop wondering who the hell had been driving that bloody car.

Four days later, Tom was back home, sitting on a reclining chair in the sunshine, in Fairholme's small rear-courtyard. He was wrapped in a thick travel blanket and was staring into space. The heavy casts he had had on his legs in the hospital had been changed for lighter ones, including the one around his crushed elbow. Liz appeared from the kitchen side door and kneeled next to him.

"What the hell happened to me, Liz?" he said in a plaintive voice. "How did all this come about?"

"That's a very long story, Tom. It will keep for now. There's plenty of time for that. You need to rest."

"Love you, Liz."

"And I love you too, Tom Cooper."

Part One – The End

Several characters in this story are based upon real people. Names and some other aspects have been changed to protect their privacy.

Part Two

Chapter One

12 September 2002

Tom sat with his feet up on a small stool in front of the gently purring log fire. He was finishing his third crossword from the small crossword book he had bought with him from the UK. These were the simple types of crosswords, not the cryptic ones favoured by his wife, Liz.

It was just after 6 pm, and dusk was settling over the area near La Manga where they had their holiday home. Come this time of the day, the temperature dropped sharply, following the sun as it fell beneath the horizon. Liz was preparing some vegetables for the evening meal which they always ate at 8 pm—whether in the UK, here in Spain or anywhere in the world for that matter.

Tom had lapsed into a warm, cosy, dream-like state, contemplating—but in truth not very hard—the answer to the clue 'Diver's weapon' (5,3), when he heard a loud and unfamiliar noise outside at the front of the house.

"What the hell was that?" said Liz, calling from the kitchen, next to the open-plan lounge and dining area.

"God alone knows," Tom shouted back. "I'll just go and see."

"Be very careful, Tom. You are still a long way from being 100%, you know."

"Don't worry, my sweetheart. Just going to look, that's all."

Tom opened the front door and was faced immediately by two men, each pointing a handgun directly at him. He tried to slam the door shut, but the larger of the two men wedged his booted foot between it and the door frame.

"Thank you for inviting us in, Dr Cooper," he said, as he pushed Tom out of the way and proceeded straight into the living room, followed by the smaller man.

"What is happening, Tom?" came the call from the kitchen.

"Stay nice and calm, Mrs Cooper. And stay just where you are," said the large man, peering into the kitchen, around the living room wall where it joined the half wall (or 'pass', as Tom and Liz called it) between the kitchen and the dining area.

Liz dropped the large metal spoon she had in her hand, screamed at the top of her voice and then shouted "TOM! TOM?"

There was no reply.

Chapter Two

Late July 2002

It was now five months since Tom had been skittled over like a pin at the end of a ten-pin bowling alley, whilst crossing the road in Leeds. He had spent just over a month in hospital; the first twelve days in the ICU—the intensive care unit. His university colleague, Jane, had suffered fewer and much less severe injuries, but she was prone to remind him at every possible chance, "I might only have had *one* broken leg; some badly bruised but not broken ribs; a sprained wrist, not a crushed elbow and some cuts and bruises here and there, but it has still changed my life you know, Dr Tom Cooper." They had been great friends at work and were now good friends out of it.

"Well, what are you going to do with yourself now you are pretty much recovered?"

"No idea," Tom said, "Maybe a break at our place in Spain for a while. Really, though, don't know yet. What about you?"

Jane poured some tea, made for them by Liz who was now busy servicing guest bedrooms of the 'B&B'.

"I'm about to start back at the university. Next week, in fact. Not my old job. That was given to an interim manager pretty soon after the…how shall I call it…'accident'. I'll be assisting him, it seems."

"As you know, Jane, I haven't recovered all my memory as yet, but one thing I do know—from Liz and others including the police—it was no bloody accident."

"Yes, OK, Tom. I do understand this whole thing has been traumatic and must feel even more so if you believe it really wasn't an accident. I seem to have been what the Americans call 'collateral damage', I think."

Her attempt at an American accent was pretty poor and to Tom, it sounded more like an Aussie or someone from South Africa.

"It WASN'T an accident, Jane. It isn't just me who believes that. The whole anti-terrorism squad at Scotland Yard believes it, and they are busy searching for the maniac who nearly killed us both."

"OK. OK. Tom. Steady on there. You'll blow a gasket if you carry on like this. Of course, I do believe you and the coppers from the Yard too. They have visited me more than once, you know, but not for a good while, I must admit."

Jane topped up her tea, and Tom's as well and helped herself to a couple of biscuits.

"Anyway, back to what you are going to do," she said whilst crunching on the small ginger nut she had just popped into her mouth.

"Don't speak with your mouth full. It is so unbecoming," Tom said in the poshest voice he could manage. Jane squirmed in her chair and started giggling like a schoolgirl who had been found out behind bike sheds with the lower sixth heartthrob.

"So, how long are you going to be away from the university?"

"Well, between us, the vice-chancellor has said my post is safe for as long as I need before I return."

"Lucky for some," said Jane through another ginger nut, "And don't go on about how much more serious your injuries were than mine—" her sentence was cut short by Liz entering the living room, plonking herself down beside Tom on the settee with a huge sigh, kicking off her shoes and saying,

"Bet, there's no tea left for one of the workers then."

"I'll go and make a fresh brew," said Tom, and before either Liz or Jane could intervene, he was off with the teapot out of the door. Jane broke the short, sort of awkward, silence, which followed Tom's departure.

"How is he doing, Liz? He's looking pretty good I would say, given what he's been through, but he says his memory isn't completely restored yet."

"His physical injuries are all but completely healed. The only slight remaining problem is his elbow. He is still getting a lot of pain with it from time to time. The surgeon was really pleased with the op, and the physio said he has made enormous progress 'for someone of his age'. She's a real turn and has been a real brick too: though Tom didn't care for the reference to his age, as you'll no doubt imagine. They can only say the pain will go away with time and plenty of exercising of the joint. No problem there, given it's the arm with which he raises his glass to drink his wine! On the other hand, the memory issue still looms *really large* for him. He gets so frustrated at not being able to recall stuff. He doesn't recognise how much progress he's made with that too. He puts so much pressure on himself. He—" Tom opened the living room door and entered with the refreshed teapot.

"Bet you've been talking about me whilst I was unavoidably detained," he said, with a twinkle in his eye.

"Now what would make you think that?" said Liz. "Actually, we've been talking about the latest article in *Woman's Own* magazine about the new crocheting styles for the spring." Jane burst into laughter, almost choking on her biscuit.

"Ha ha. Very funny," said Tom as he poured the tea. "So, where did you get to? My memory, I bet."

"I was about to explain that more or less, 70% of your memory has returned, but you still pressurise yourself about the other 30%. The doctors have told you that the more you do that, the slower it will be to return. You know," she said, looking at Jane, "a bit like desperately trying to remember the name of a place you visited and finding it pops into your head when you are thinking about something else completely? It will take time, Tom. But you carry on bashing your head against that wall over there because for you, it is taking too much time."

"I know! I know!" said Tom, exasperated at his own failure.

Just at that moment, the front doorbell rang. "Another waif and stray looking for a room for the night, I wouldn't wonder," said Tom, getting up to go and see.

"Well, well, well," Liz said, standing up as the visitor and Tom came into the living room. "DCI Williams. It's been a while."

"Yes, it has Mrs Cooper. And good to see you too, Ms Carter. Maybe I am going to be able to kill two birds, as the saying goes." As soon as the words had left his lips, he knew it wasn't the best old saying to use in this situation. "Sorry, I simply meant…"

"No need to apologise," said Tom, sitting down beside Liz. "We all know it wasn't meant to offend, though it was a tad unfortunate. Anyway, what can we do for you?" he said, whilst directing the DCI to the armchair opposite him and Liz.

"We've been working hard behind the scenes Tom, and I have here some photos which might include one of the BMW drivers." He fumbled in the old and tired-looking brown briefcase, which he had deposited on the floor beside his chair and pulled out a beige-coloured file, labelled: 'Tom Cooper/ Jane Carter—Suspects'. "I was wondering if you and—as you are here, you too, Ms Carter—would look at them to see if anything stirs any kind of memory of the driver that day? We have side-view shots of each of them as well."

"No harm in looking," Tom said, in a resigned 'I won't remember anything' tone of voice, which produced a gentle dig in his ribs from Liz. "Hey, that hurt; you vicious woman."

"No, it didn't. Now behave, Dr Cooper, and help DCI Williams."

"OK. But one thing before we look at the file if I may, DCI Williams."

"Of course, Tom. What is it?"

"Well, the last time we met, you said you were investigating the number of the car to see if it gave you any leads. Have you found any?"

"Sorry, Tom. I thought I had told you already. Good job; I have this 'ere notebook, given I cannot remember my own name some days. Failed me today, though. Anyway, the eyewitness reports we have confirmed that the rear number plate was covered-up and there was a temporary red and white plate in the rear window. The front plate was damaged in the collision and no one seems to have seen it before it ran into you. Anyway, the red and white plate doesn't match any that have been issued under licence. A fake number plate, you'll be surprised to know," he said, with more than a hint of sarcasm in his voice.

"OK. Tell you what, it will be easier if Jane and I go into the breakfast room and use the table in there to look at the file."

Tom turned page after page, and nothing seemed to bring back any memories of the person driving the car. "This is hopeless," said Jane, "I didn't even know it was a BMW until a few weeks ago, let alone what the driver looked like. I never really saw him."

Tom was staring, eyes wide, with eyeballs like old fashioned 'gob-stoppers' that he used to buy from the local shop when he was a boy while staying with his grandparents on Saturday afternoons.

"Have you spotted someone?" Jane said, sounding more concerned than excited.

"We need to go right through the file to the end," Tom said in a somewhat distant voice, whilst turning the next page. DCI Williams and Liz finally moved through to the breakfast room, having decided to give Jane and Tom some space to consider the pictures.

"Well, Tom? Ms Carter? Any luck?"

"Please, do call me Jane. Sorry, but I didn't see anyone I recognised, let alone someone who might have been driving the car."

"Thank you, Ms Car…er…I mean, Jane. And you, Tom?"

"I recognise this one," he said, pointing to a picture at the bottom of the eighth page of the file.

"Thanks, Tom. Well, I better be going. I'll be in touch again in the next few weeks." DCI Williams got up, shook everyone's hand and left.

Jane had meant to be back home at least half-an-hour ago, but she just had to find out who was the bloody nutter who had nearly killed her.

"Well," said Liz, "who in God's name did you see?"

Although it was only 4:30 in the afternoon, Tom poured himself a very large glass of Shiraz and stood to look out of the bay window of the sitting room.

"Well, Tom?" said Liz, clearly exasperated.

"It was Monika. Monika von Strauss."

"I need a drink too."

"I'll get you one," Tom said as he crossed the sitting room.

"Make it a big one."

"Do you want something, Jane?"

"Thanks, but I only drink when I'm celebrating something or feel really happy for some other reason. Doesn't feel like this fits either bill, somehow."

Liz and Jane joined Tom in the breakfast room as he was on his way through it to the sitting room, from the kitchen. They all sat down at the breakfast room table, hardly able to contemplate what Tom had seen.

"So," said Liz, "the woman you once lived with in Germany; who presumably once loved you; now tries to kill you."

"Well, she was in that file of suspects, and I don't think Charlie Farley was playing games, do you?"

"We shouldn't call him that. One day we'll forget ourselves and call him that to his face. I quite like him. He seems to care." Jane couldn't help but laugh at the use of the nickname, remembering the diminutive, bumbling sleuth played, to hilarious effect, by Ernie Wise when she had seen repeats of the famous *Morecambe and Wise Saturday Night* shows in the nineties.

"Whatever, whatever." It was Tom's turn to be exasperated. "The key question is: *Was* she the driver? If she

100

was, then she knew where Jane and I would be that day. She knew our route to the train station and the time at which we would probably be crossing that road." Tom topped up his glass, got up from the table and started pacing up and down. "That means she almost certainly knows where we both work."

"But we've said all this before, Tom. *Whoever* was driving would need to know those things," Liz said, finishing her glass and pouring another.

Jane had stopped laughing or even smiling. "So, she could come and try to get us again," she said, her hands resting on the table and visibly trembling. "I start back to work next week. What am I going to do, Tom? What am I going to do?" There was more than a hint of panic in the question and her voice.

"I need to call Charlie," he said dryly. The following morning, he made the call.

"Detective Inspector Williams. What can I do for you?" he said at the end of a crackly landline.

"It's Tom, Tom Cooper here," he said, his voice trembling slightly. "I need to speak to you about what I saw yesterday afternoon."

"I guessed you would, Tom, but the phone isn't wise. We need to meet. Can I suggest the place where you met my colleague Commander Fitzsimmons some time ago?"

"You can, but I can't remember where that was. It's part of my memory which hasn't returned yet."

"Ah. OK. Will your wife remember, perhaps?"

"I'm sure she will. What day and time?"

"Sounds pretty urgent by the nature of your voice, Tom. How about tomorrow at 6 pm?"

"Great. See you tomorrow. And…er…many thanks."

Chapter Three

Just like the last time, Tom arrived first. The bar, near the side entrance to the station, was bustling and very noisy, not at all like the last time he was there. He pushed his way to the bar, ordered a large red wine and found a seat in the far-right corner—away from the noise as far as he could get. "That's lucky," he murmured in doing so, reminding himself of a dear friend from Devon who was always saying this and who lived not far from their holiday home in Spain where Tom had first met him. It was the only table left unoccupied and, by good fortune, probably the best one for the conversation he hoped to have with DCI Williams.

It was now 6:30 and still no sign of the DCI. He thought about calling his number at the Yard, but they probably wouldn't know where he was if 'Charlie' was still on his way to meet him. He asked a young man sitting nearby if he would keep an eye on his seat, whilst he went to the bar.

"No problem," the young man said in a broad Irish accent. After a scramble to even reach the bar, let alone get a drink, Tom eventually pushed his way through the crowd back to his seat.

"Thanks," he said to the young man, "pretty damned full in here tonight, eh?"

"Aye. Always like this when *United* are playing at home—well, at least just before and for a while after the match, such as now," he said.

"By the sound and look of it, I guess they must have won," said Tom in a sort of question-come-statement tone of voice.

"Yep. Beat the Baggies, 3-1."

"Of course! I'd completely forgotten it was today. *West Brom* is my home team. Thought we might get a bit of a pasting today, mind you. Were you at the match, then?" asked Tom.

"No, I've been at work all day," said the young Irishman, just as DCI Williams appeared through the crowd.

"At last," said Tom. "Where on earth have you been all this time?"

"Got caught up in another case before I could leave the Yard I'm afraid, Tom. Anyway, I'm here now. Let's get down to business."

"Let me get you a drink at least," Tom said, somewhat apologetically, having remembered it was he who asked for the meeting.

"I'm fine. Let's just press on. What is it you wanted to talk to me about?"

"Well, you'll know the photo I pointed out was Monika von Strauss and that I once lived with her in the seventies at the time of the incident I had with the briefcase in Bonn. You will also know that the briefcase was meant to get to her via me acting like an innocent courier."

"Yes, Tom. We know all this. Now please get to what it is you *really* want to tell me."

"Well, I bet you don't know that when I knew her, she had a fear of driving. No licence and wasn't about to try and get one no matter what anyone said." Tom waited for some sort of reaction. Williams didn't move a muscle. "So, it couldn't have been her driving that bloody BMW."

"Well, we can all get over our fears, Tom, and in any event, you are talking about a time over a quarter of a century ago when you and her lived together. People change."

"Maybe, but are you seriously telling me that someone who had a morbid fear of driving all her life overcomes that sufficiently well to be driving a left-hand drive BMW, at break-neck (or legs) speed around a sharp 90-degree right-hand bend, in a country which drives on the wrong side of the road from her point of view; hits two pedestrians and still has the skill and nerve to carry on down the road 'as if nothing has happened', as you told me one of your eyewitnesses described it." Tom suddenly realised what he had said. He had recalled the car being left-hand drive; something he had not been able to remember before. The point wasn't lost on DCI Williams.

"Whether your speculation is correct or not, Tom, the fact you now seem to know it was a left-hand drive car is a huge bonus for you and for me. First, a fragment of your lost memory has just returned. Second, we can now seriously narrow our search for the car. Our eyewitnesses gave conflicting reports about whether it was right or left-hand drive." He stood up to go. "I need to get back."

"But I need to ask you something before you go," said Tom, assertively. "Whoever was driving that damn car, Monika or another mad idiot, they must have known Jane and me—well, me at least—would be there and at roughly that time. That means they must know where we work and knew of the meeting we were attending and where it was being held. Jane starts working at the university again next week. She is petrified. What can you do?"

DCI Williams lent forward, palms down on the table and whispered in Tom's right ear, "Tom, you and Ms Carter...er...Jane, have had round-the-clock plain-clothed police and special branch protection since the day you both left the hospital. That will continue until we find the person or persons responsible for your injuries. Now, I must be on my way. It has been good to see you again. I will be in touch." And with that, he turned and disappeared through the crowd and out of the bar.

On his way home, Tom couldn't get out of his mind the thought that someone was watching him day and night—and presumably Liz too—but he'd been leaning on the table in the bar for far too long, and now his elbow ached like hell. While he massaged it and swallowed two Paracetamol with the tea he'd bought from a kiosk in the station, he wondered what Liz would make of the fact they had 'a minder'.

He hadn't been home very long and was in the middle of telling her all about the meeting with 'Charlie Farley' when the doorbell rang. "Bugger," said Liz, as she got up and went to the front door. It was Des and Anne, their near neighbours who also ran a guesthouse.

"Just popping in to see how the wounded soldier is today." Des said in his now-familiar Yorkshire drawl which reminded Liz a bit of 'Charlie Farley'.

Tom turned around as the pair came into the breakfast room followed by Liz.

"He was just telling me about his meeting today with DCI Williams." They all sat around the table. "Go on Tom, finish what you were telling me," said Liz.

"Well, the upshot is that the driver of said BMW couldn't have been Monika because she had a morbid fear of driving. And even if she had somehow overcome it—as Charlie suggested she could have—I don't believe she could have driven a left-hand drive car the way it was driven around that corner, into Jane and me, and then carried on as if nothing had happened."

"Listen, you two. You've clearly got lots to talk about, and we only popped-in briefly on our way to town to get a few things," said Anne, getting up and moving towards the breakfast room door.

"Why don't you come to us later for a bite of supper?" said Des. "Nothing fancy. Probably one of Anne's beef casseroles; a bit like cassoulet, but with beef rather than pork. What do you say?"

Tom looked at Liz who nodded and said, "Sounds good. We can also pick your brains about the latest thinking on Tom's incident."

"Excellent," said Des, joining Anne who was now almost at the front door. "8:30 or thereabouts, OK?"

"Great."

Chapter Four

August 2002

Anne and Des' own accommodation in their guesthouse was nothing like the comfortable arrangements Tom and Liz had in theirs. In effect, they lived in a room which was like a bedsit—one room with a bed and small table, and with a small kitchen or 'kitchenette' as they were sometimes called, accessed through a doorless 'doorway'.

Their hallway was half taken-up by the reception desk and reception area packed with tourist information leaflets about what to see and do in the town and local area. The equivalent to Tom and Liz's sitting room was a dedicated breakfast room for the paying guests. They had seven letting rooms, making it much busier and generally noisier than Liz's relatively peaceful two-room set-up. Despite the idea that 'Bed and Breakfast' meant just that—you stayed out of the place after breakfast and until bedtime—people came and went pretty much all the time—or it seemed that way—which was often wearing on Anne and Des. Still, according to 'Trip Advisor'—the bane of every B&B owner's life—it was one of the most popular B&Bs in the whole of the town, and Des and Anne's grand plan was to make enough money to eventually sell it, and move on to a more peaceful, less tying and trying existence, possibly on the coast…but not to run a B&B!

Tom and Anne arrived closer to 9 o'clock than 8:30 pm, delayed by calls for room bookings. Tom presented Des with a bottle of Chilean Malbec—one of Tom's absolute favourite tipples—and there were some flowers for Anne. All very traditional, and probably considered sexist by some. As would also be the fact that it was Liz who immediately went to the kitchenette to see if Anne needed any help with the meal. Des poured drinks; Liz and Anne emerged fairly quickly from attending to the meal, to join them.

"When I was in town today, I was wondering whether there were any eyewitness reports of what happened, and what they had said about the driver," said Des, cradling his glass of Malbec and 'drinking in' it's wonderful bouquet. "You've never mentioned such reports."

"Well, according to DCI Williams," said Liz, "there had been conflicting statements from them. Some seemed to think it was a right-hand drive and others that it was left-hand drive. Don't know if they mentioned whether it was a man or woman. Did he mention that to you, Tom?"

"No, he didn't come to think of it. But then I guess he would have ruled out of court my conversation with him about Monika if he had evidence; it was definitely a man. Maybe the eyewitnesses weren't sure. Monika's picture showed her with pretty, short hair."

"Or maybe there were two people in the car which is why the witnesses gave different accounts of where the driver was sitting," said Anne, getting up to check the casserole again.

"Bloody hell," said Tom. "I hadn't thought of that, and 'Charlie Farley' has never mentioned it to me either." Des got up, topped up his and Tom's glasses with the Malbec. "I suppose it could have been anyone but now I think of it, there wasn't a picture of Declan Brophy or van Voet in the file, so they must be ruling them out as suspects."

Tom had decided that he ought to tell Anne and Des about the minder he had, just in case they saw anyone acting suspiciously in the street. He had told Liz earlier and she had heaved a huge sigh of relief at the news. He told them over the truly delicious casserole.

"God, Tom. Do you know what this minder looks like?" Anne asked with a worried look on her face.

"No, not really. But since Charlie told me I have been wondering about how it was that I got the only free table in the station bar—and one in a sort of private corner—when the

107

place was heaving with folks. The guy sat at the next table was young—I'd say in his late twenties or early thirties—and seemed happy enough to watch my seat and my bag when I went to the bar. He had a very thick Irish accent which, these days, tends to make me a bit nervous even if some might say there's probably no need. He just sat there doing a crossword or Sudoku or something in his newspaper. But now, I wonder if he was my minder; knew Charlie was coming to meet me, and somehow kept the table free for me. Charlie and he never exchanged even so much as a glance, which I suppose makes sense if he was a complete stranger or even if he was our minder."

"I bet he'd been sitting at your table, to keep it free for you and Charlie Farley until he saw you coming into the bar," Des said a bit limply.

"Then, he'd still have the problem of keeping *his* table free for when Tom or Charlie arrived," Liz said, thinking Des might have had too much wine to be offering such a lame comment.

"Or maybe, Charlie didn't know him even if he was your minder," said Anne. "He could have been special branch from what you said DCI Williams had said."

It had never been the idea for the evening to go into the small hours but it was already 11:00 and everyone was well aware that, except for Tom, they all had busy days tomorrow.

"Time we were off," said Liz, giving Tom a nudge.

"Yes, absolutely. The workers need their rest so they can keep me in the luxury to which I have become accustomed."

"It's been a lovely evening," Liz said, "and that casserole is absolutely wonderful, Anne. Can I have the recipe or is it a family secret?"

"You are welcome to have it, Liz, but we'll probably have to kill you once you have it," said Des, grinning from ear to ear and clearly not realising what he had said.

"You mindless oaf!" Anne shouted at him, as she handed Liz and Tom their light summer coats. "What kind of a thing is that to say given what we've been talking about all evening, and what happened to Tom and all that."

"Oh, God. I am so sorry, Tom. I didn't think. I didn't mean…er…I didn't…" he burbled.

"No problem, Des. Forget it. No harm done. Or, as Liz is fond of saying 'no one died, did they'?"

Tom and Liz walked the short way down the street to Fairholme. When they opened the door, there was a small white envelope on the porch doormat.

"What's this?" Tom said, examining the envelope as they walked through the inner door, down the hallway and into the breakfast room. You didn't need to be Sherlock Holmes to quickly realise it must have been hand-delivered as it didn't have a postage stamp or postmark, and in any event, the post wouldn't be delivered between 7 pm and 11 pm. "Don't recognise the writing. Do you Liz?"

"No. But do you think you should open it, Tom? Remember Jane's fear of 'them' knowing where you and she worked. If 'they' know that, then they can know where we live." Tom stood looking at the envelope, feeling across its front and back and around its edges to see if he might feel some wires or such like.

"It could have been left by our minder, Liz. Anyway, I can't feel anything untoward inside, but you go into the living room and close the door, will you? Just to be on the safe side."

"If you're going to die, then I will go with you." Her voice was determined and loving all at the same time.

Tom pulled a knife from the kitchen cutlery drawer and slit the envelope across the top edge. No bang. He took out a single sheet of lined A4 notepaper. He unfolded it. The message, in capital letters, read:

YOU WON'T KNOW WHEN IT WILL COME, BUT
WE WILL GET YOU AND THIS TIME, WE WON'T
MISS.
YOUR MINDER WILL BE NO USE AT ALL

Tom tossed the paper across the table, put his head in his hands and said quietly, "When is this all going to end, Liz? When will it end?"

The following morning, Tom was up much earlier than usual to help Liz with the breakfast. They danced around each other, ferrying plates, dishes, cutlery and all the other stuff for a full English breakfast, in complete silence. Had it been any other day, Tom and Liz might have been stifling the repeated urge to giggle like naughty schoolchildren.

They were serving a Welsh couple who had asked, on arrival two days ago, if it was safe to drink the water from the taps. When Liz had relayed the story, Tom burst into uncontrolled laughter, spluttering in reply, "Where do they think they are staying, for God's sake? Somewhere in the middle of the jungle? Don't they know this is England in the twenty-first century?"

But it wasn't just another day.

During the night, Tom had tossed and turned and slept very little. Everything that had gone on kept swirling around his head. In the end, he made his mind up that they were going to stay for a while in their Spanish home. Bugger the people booked to stay in the B&B; Liz would just have to relocate them to other guesthouses belonging to several owners she knew who were known collectively as the 'B&B mafia'.

That morning, he spelt out his plan to Liz whilst they were clearing away the debris from the Welsh couple's breakfast. She complied immediately, realising only too well that this made great sense. She was joyously relieved. Only immediate family and close friends knew of their place down in Cabo de Palos: a small and, for much of the year, a quiet coastal village with a working fishing harbour and marina, not far from La Manga. She could already imagine them sitting for coffee at 'Bouquets', their favourite café and *panadería* on the harbour front, overlooking the small sea wall with an uninterrupted sea view beyond; or having a meal at the 'Miramar' on the corner of the harbour and marina. Bliss.

Liz spent that morning on the phone, relocating her booked guests and then informing them. Some had no problem and replied with the usual, polite "Thank you for letting us know". Others were less understanding and required a few inducements, such as 'free tickets to the Railway

Museum', which Liz chose not to explain, is free entry anyway.

Tom spent his morning booking their flights. Normally, they would book return flights, but this time Tom decided it was better to leave that decision until they felt better about returning to the UK and to Fairholme. Liz had relocated guests for the next three weeks, but if they needed to stay in Spain longer, then she could rearrange guest bookings by email or on the phone with her friends in the 'B&B mafia'.

Finally, Tom decided he should call 'Charlie Farley' and let him know what they were doing.

"I'm not sure this is a good plan, Tom. You'll be out of our jurisdiction for one thing. And for another, you won't have your own support network around you should you need it."

"We have friends down there if we need them," Tom said indignantly. "And anyway, we are not expecting to need support like that. No doubt you'll be in touch if we need to be alerted to any problems?" Tom never mentioned the 'minder' and neither did DCI Williams.

"We will, Tom. Be assured, we will. Have a good holiday."

.

Chapter Five

DCI Charlie Williams had called another case meeting. DS Henderson and DC Swain came into the room. DC Ali—known as Naz to everyone in the station—was in charge of basic case notes and organising meetings and was already in the room when they arrived. They sat around the table in one of the anonymous, small, grey meeting rooms of which there were so many at The Met.

"So, what you got for us, Naz?" said Williams.

"Well, not a lot really since our last briefing, guv," he said in a low and clearly nervous tone. "We're now tracking all left-hand drive BMW 3 series known to DVLA. We've continued our searches into the financial records of the companies and their directors, whom we listed at our last meeting. So far, nothing really positive to report on any of these counts from the records, but I think DC Swain might have an update on that from just this morning."

"OK. But let's focus on the car for a minute. What have you two on that?" he said, pointing at Swain and Henderson.

"Nothing yet on the BMW, well…er…not of the right model, age or colour. We—" Swain's report was cut short by an unusually angry DCI rising from behind his desk and slamming his fist on the top of it as he did so.

"Bugger the bloody colour. As I think you know as well as me, cars can be resprayed. Yes?"

"Yes, sir."

"And, how far are we searching for this damn car? Nationwide, I assume? Involving other forces too? Tell me I am right."

"You are, sir. We are covering all leads from DVLA but..."

"But what, DC Swain?"

"Well, if I might say, it seems such a waste of time with the resources we have. Wouldn't we be better focusing all our effort on those funding this?"

"Go on."

"Well, you know, we could spend weeks and weeks looking for a car that has been so changed we might never be able to link it to the scene of the crime. Probably in a breaker's yard soon after it was used, anyway. And almost certainly nicked unless, of course, this was a genuine accident and not the work of a hit squad."

"I don't think even the worst motorist in the world drives through a red-light at the reported speed this one did—wheels squealing, back-end sliding, etc—slams into two pedestrians like they are bits of kindling and then skilfully drives away as if nothing has happened. Nothing about this adds up to an accident. More like an expert driver skilled in this type of thing. What do you think, Henderson?"

"It's the speed of the vehicle which makes me come down on the side of a deliberate attempt to take these two people out, sir."

Swain looked down at her shoes, deflated written all over her face. "Why the hell did I mention it might just be an accident after all?" she said to herself.

"So, what more do we have on the possible people behind this, since last time we all met together? Naz?"

"Nothing really positive except one small possibility which might be worth pursuing, sir."

"C'mon then, spit it out," said Williams, genuinely exasperated at how long all this was taking.

"One company director we have been tracking—Luciano Copa—might have had connections to the mafia and the IRA in the early seventies. Nothing is really clear at all, but Interpol believes he was somehow linked—possibly financially—to one or both."

"What makes them think all this? And who the hell is he, anyway?"

"He made his money initially in the steel business," interrupted Henderson.

"Is that 's-t-e-e-l' or 's-t-e-a-l'?" said Swain, grinning from ear to ear; desperately trying to rescue her reputation with the governor.

"Yeh, yeh, very droll," said Henderson. "Round of applause for the hilarious DC."

"Stop pissing about you two. Answer my question." Williams was definitely not amused.

Henderson sat up straighter and began.

"Copa was a steel magnate in Milan in the late sixties. His family were staunch right-wing Republicans, as was he. He stood for election in 1968 and got in. It was the year Mariano Rumor led the Christian Democrats to a resounding victory over the Communists. Alongside his national government work, he continued to play a huge part in city politics throughout the seventies. It is claimed that during this time, he became friendly with senior mafia figures and, through them, possibly with key players in the IRA. Evidence is sketchy, but it's known he and his family met at least two senior mafia figures and their families on holiday, at least twice. Just good friends, perhaps? Maybe. But Interpol is convinced he bankrolled two or even three large jobs for the mafia and maybe the IRA during this time and afterwards."

"Listen. I've heard all this before the last time we met for a CC. What the hell is new for God's sake? Tell me something I haven't heard a dozen times."

"Well," said Henderson, "We now know that Interpol has managed to get an ex-copper from the Italian police into a position as Copa's driver and main security guard. And he's picked up something that might interest us."

"Spit it out. C'mon, I haven't got all day." Williams was on edge which was very unlike him, thought Naz.

"The intel is that there's a job going down somewhere in the UK after a bungled one sometime ago. This time one of Luciano's own hitmen is doing the work. Luciano is financing the hit," said Henderson. He looked across at Swain, who he could see was physically trembling.

"Anything else?"

"No, sir."

Williams got up from his chair, walked towards the small, high window behind him, and then spun around coming forward so as to lean on the back of his chair, looking directly at Swain and Henderson on the opposite side of the table.

"Well, for a start, it would seem that Signore Copa is sufficiently worried that he's prepared to send his own trusted hit-man to do this job. That must mean he's implicated somehow, someway, and seriously, in whatever 'the mark' knows. Yes?"

They all nodded.

"OK. First, we need to ask if our Italian ex-copper can find out who was driving the car that nearly did for Cooper and Carter. Second, we need to try and get more details about Signore Copa's trusted hitman. Anything at all will help. The basic connections are too close to ignore but we need more detail. In the meantime, I'm going upstairs to brief the gaffer. You two better make sure your passports are valid and you're ready for a trip. Thanks, everyone."

They all filed out of the room. As he left, Naz's shoulders slumped. He wondered once again how long it was going to be before he did some proper detective work rather than shuffle files and notes around, either on his computer or in paper, or summarise what he'd been told by others. He had been 'made up'—as promotion is generally called in the force—for a few years now.

"Your time will come," came a whisper in his right ear. It was DCI Williams.

"Oh. Yes, sir. I know…"

"That's not it, Naz. You wouldn't want this assignment however long you'd been a DC. However, you may be needed on the ground, whether ready or not. So, be sure you are."

Naz walked down the corridor and back to his desk wondering what on earth that meant.

Chapter Six

Late on 12 September 2002

"Just come out of the kitchen, Mrs Cooper, and come and sit on the settee in your living room," said the large man gesturing to her with his pistol. "You have nothing to fear."

Liz walked slowly out of the kitchen and passed the large man. She was trembling all over. She could immediately see Tom sat at one end of the corner settee with some tape over his mouth, with a man stood over him, pistol aimed at him. She went to sit down next to Tom, but the larger man guided her to sit at the opposite end of the corner settee.

Just as she began to speak, the larger man intervened.

"OK, Dr and Mrs Cooper. This has been a traumatic few minutes for you. But in our view, we had few alternatives but to do this. We could not afford great long conversations on your doorstep about who we were, showing our IDs, and explaining what we were doing here. We had no idea if there were people in the next house to you or if others opposite might hear. Our best chance of making it quickly inside was to stun you into this situation and take it from there."

"And anyone staying with us would be blown away with us, I suppose? Fine. Just dandy. So, who the bloody hell are you? Come to blow out our brains and scarper? Job well done? OK. So, here you go. Here's my temple for you to have shooting practice at." Liz turned sideways so she was looking directly at Tom and her right temple faced the gun, which was held a short way from her head. To say 'Liz was not amused' would be an understatement. To say 'She was behaving recklessly' would be an even bigger one.

"There are those who want to do that, Mrs Cooper." He dropped his gun and signalled to his colleague to do the same. "I am Detective Sergeant Henderson, and my colleague over there is DC Swain. We work with DCI Williams at The Met. Here are our IDs. We will explain everything." At that, DC Swain took off the woolly hat she had been wearing, revealing her hair tied in a knot on top of her head. She untied it and her hair fell casually onto her shoulders.

"Good God. A woman!" Liz exclaimed. Liz looked at their ID cards and then slumped back into the settee. "Having another woman on the scene certainly makes me feel a little bit easier. Right, now take that bloody tape from Tom's mouth."

Tom yelped as the 'gaffer' tape ripped off bits of his stubble. It wasn't loud and the pain was gone as soon as it came.

"So, first of all, what the hell are you doing here?" he said. "Second, how did you manage to get guns through all the screening at the airports? Third, why are you two here and not Charlie F—"

"DCI Charlie Williams," Liz interjected, scowling at Tom. She just knew using that nickname had become too routine.

"If you were going to say 'Charlie Farley', Mr Cooper, then don't feel too bad. When the DCI first joined the Met, we had a raffle to decide his nickname. 'Charlie Farley' was one of the choices. However, 'Barnsley Charlie' won the day—he is originally from Barnsley, you see. And 'Barnsley Charlie' is how he is known to all his colleagues, though naturally never to his face."

Tom managed a stifled chuckle, and so did Liz. Henderson and Swain laughed out loud. The tension you would have previously needed an axe to cut, suddenly fell away.

"Maybe I could take your questions a little out of order, Mr Cooper?"

Tom nodded as he continued to rub and scratch his stubble where the tape had once been.

"We didn't bring these guns through any airport. We had prearranged to collect them from our colleagues in the CNI— the *Centro Nacional de Inteligencia,* which is something like our special branch and MI6 rolled into one—on our way from the airport to here and after first collecting our hire car. We met them not far from here in a place called Los Belones."

Tom suddenly felt the need for a drink. "I'm going to have a large glass of my favourite Shiraz. What would anyone else like?"

"*Para mí, uno grande vino blanco, por favor señor,*" said Liz, with a huge and knowing grin.

"I'm afraid only one of us can have alcohol at any one time. One of us has to be fully in command of their senses and their wits. Do you want something, Laura?" Henderson said, looking at her, now seated next to Tom.

"The same as Mrs Cooper would be great."

"If I could have some water and a cup of tea that would be great," Henderson said, stoically.

"Coming up," Tom said.

He went on, "Well, since we are cast together like this, it would be friendlier to use first names all around, don't you think? You must know by now that we are Tom and Liz and we now know you are Laura. So, DS Henderson?"

"I'm Gavin. And before anyway says it, no, I'm not the former international rugby union player," he said with a grimace. "You can't imagine how many times I've been asked that. He was Gavin Henson, not Henderson. Anyway, back to your questions, Tom. As to what we are doing here, that is indeed a long story. Anyway, here goes with the shorter version, to begin with." He had by now sat down on the pouffe near the television in the corner of the room, looking at the other three on the corner settee across the coffee table.

"Our plan is for the four of us to drive back to the UK through Spain and France and north to your home. We now believe we know why the note pushed through your door, and which you sent to DCI Williams, said that your minder 'will be no use at all'. The assassin or assassins will attempt to…how shall I say…er…bump you off, inside your house, having registered as a paying guest in the B&B." He gulped down half a glass of water and took a good sip of his tea.

"DCI Williams' idea is that Laura and I, posing as a couple, will occupy one of your rooms for a few days after we get back. Other officers will replace us after that. You won't let your other room at all until you get the all-clear from us about who is trying to book it. At some point, the assassins will try to book it and you will let them."

By now both Tom and Liz were looking very pale, feeling sick and bewildered. Tom had moved to sit close to Liz. He put one arm around her shoulders and drained his glass using the other. Tom started the interrogation.

"So, you're going to use us as bait. Like bloody worms on the end of a sodding hook; dangling before them so they can blast us into kingdom come; all nice set up by you and Barnsley bugger lugs and no doubt the big wigs at Scotland Yard." Tom was incandescent.

"Well, if you think we're just going to say 'Oh, thank you very much, kind sir; we are so grateful', then you better bloody think again. And, what's more, you just better have tickets for the next plane out of here tomorrow. There's a decent small hotel just down the road. I'll show you…NOW!"

He stood up and walked around the coffee table, banging unforgivingly into Swain's knees as he did so, toward the front door. He opened it and gestured Henderson out through it.

Neither Henderson nor Swain moved from their seats.

"C'mon, c'mon. Out you go. The hotel isn't far. You can walk it in less than 10 minutes."

Henderson and Swain sat still. Swain was watching Liz very closely. Henderson's eyes were fixed on Tom.

"OK. Then I'll call 112 and get the police here."

"And what will you say to them, Dr Cooper? You're being held against your will by two UK police officers? You've been kidnapped by two UK police officers? Two UK police officers are planning to return you to the UK against your will? What will it be?" Henderson's tone was steady and resolute.

Liz looked very pale now and very upset, but through the tears rolling gently down her cheeks she could only think of one thing—the note they had found on their doormat back at Fairholme.

"I know exactly how it feels just now, my sweetheart," she said, looking unblinkingly straight into Tom's eyes. "But do you remember how we felt when we read that note left on our doormat? Do you remember asking me 'when will it all end?' I think we have a chance to draw a line in the sand under all of this and gain our lives back again. We seem to have a small army working to achieve that. It's got to be worth a shot at it, hasn't it?"

Tom stood half in and half out of the front door, staring back at Liz and wondering where the hell all that strength had come from. For his own part, he felt like the quivering wreck that he was. He looked at Swain, then at Henderson. They seemed genuine people, but then again, they were just doing their job. Liz was probably right. A kind of all-or-nothing strategy and the tactic to achieve it that the Met was using wasn't unlike some he'd used at the university to get closer to achieving an important goal. He remembered one time when it was to get staff to go along with the new way of designing curricula which they were absolutely set against. Suddenly, a small gust of cool night air brought him back to the present. He looked again at Liz, whose expression was 'for God's sake, we have to do this'.

He closed the door.

"All right." The release of tension in the room was palpable. "But on one condition."

Henderson and Swain looked at each other, and Liz looked questioningly at Tom, stood by the front door.

"You stop using the 'a-word'."

Liz broke into almost hysterical laughter and Swain followed not too far behind. Henderson smiled, as if to himself rather than to anyone else.

"We have become so used to thinking of them like that, Tom. We are both really sorry about using it here," said Swain, through tears of laughter.

"Yes, very sorry, Tom. And to you too, Liz," said Henderson. "How about attackers, or intruders?"

"How about bastards," said Liz through her tears of relief. Tom laughed that nervous laugh, any of us capable of laughing in this situation would have had.

"Bastards it is," said Tom, walking back to the coffee table and offering his hand to Henderson and then to Swain. They shook hands to seal the deal. And they all knew this was not just about what to call the assassins. He sat down next to Liz, put his arm around her shoulder and gave her a lasting and loving hug. Silence fell for more than a moment, broken only by the comforting sound of wood crackling on the fire.

Eventually, Tom said, "So, tell me, why is the plan to drive back to the UK? We can get really cheap air tickets here and not just if you book them months in advance. We could fly out of Malaga or San Javier."

"The idea," Swain started, "is to give our guys back at the Met time to pair up appropriate colleagues who can act as couples staying for a few days at your lovely B&B and to see York. It will take time to sort all that out."

"And in addition," Henderson continued, "we need time for our bugging expert to bug your house so we, or any of our colleagues, can keep tabs on what the bastards are planning."

Tom got up to pour himself, Liz and Laura more wine. Henderson took the chance to go to the toilet and, at the same time, have a very brief sneaky look at that part of the rest of the house and in particular, the level of security. When they were all back together again, Tom said,

"I imagine the idea is to drive our car back to the UK? Presumably, your hire car has to be returned pretty soon."

"Exactly, Tom," Henderson said. "We have the option to return our car to the local police here in Cabo de Palos either tomorrow or the day after. They'll sort things out with the hiring company. In any case, we thought you and Liz would be more familiar with driving on the right, and the vast majority of the journey will be like that."

"Makes sense, I suppose," Liz said in a very weary voice, "but remember, it might be re-registered though it's still right-hand drive."

"I think it's time for us to show our guests where they will be sleeping," said Tom, getting up from the settee.

Chapter Seven

Maybe Laura and Gavin knew, or maybe they didn't, but thankfully, Liz and Tom's house in Spain could easily accommodate four adults sleeping—even if two of the four wouldn't be sleeping in the same bed or bedroom. Laura was going to sleep in the original main bedroom opposite the main house bathroom; and Gavin in the original second one, almost adjacent through another door. Tom and Liz slept at the other end of the house, upstairs in the extension built by the previous owner, and with their own en suite below, down two short flights of stairs.

After it was all quiet in the house, Swain, as previously agreed, gently knocked on the door to Henderson's room, and they began a short check on what they needed to do.

"They're both really on edge," said Swain, "She's been like this now pretty much since we arrived. He was obviously stressed out when he went to the door this evening but seems a bit more relaxed now, but still very touchy I'd say."

"Yep. Absolutely agree. You need to try and reassure her as often as possible, and I'll do the same with him. Apart from that, all we have to do now is to check-in with the boss and confirm all our plans."

"And, what about all this sharing our histories? They'd have dicky-fits if they heard mine," said Swain.

"No one ever said they have to be factually accurate. Make it up. You've been pretty damn good at that in recent years as far as I hear."

Swain took a huge swipe at him but missed by a mile and landed face down on the bed.

"Serves you right," he said, turning her over, straddling her, and peering into her dark blue eyes. "Time for bed, I think. And remember to be back next door before they come down this way." A comment which earned him a knee in the groin, which *did* find its mark.

Whatever was happening at the other end of the house, neither Liz nor Tom slept well. In fact, they were both awake long before their usual time for rising, especially here in Spain. Liz decided that Laura and Gavin would probably welcome a traditional English breakfast—one such as she might prepare in the B&B, and which always received rave reviews. The smell of bacon sizzling in the pan was too much for Gavin, even though he felt as if he could—and probably should—have slept for much longer. There was no sign of Laura.

The house was regularly described by those who first saw it as a 'Tardis'—the outwardly small, old-fashioned, police box still used in the UK TV sci-fi programme, *Doctor Who*, but which turned out to be much larger once you were inside.

The house had potentially five bedrooms, though the smallest had been commandeered by Tom as his study, and the next largest by Liz as her sewing and ironing room and also as a place to store stuff like cushions for the loungers and for the chairs around the table on the front terrace; umbrellas for one of the tables on the rear terrace; gas bottles for the BBQ. It was the equivalent of the junk space under the stairs which most people have in two-storey houses in Britain and many other parts of the West in Liz's experience.

Tom, Liz and Gavin were about to sit down to breakfast. The coffee machine had been bubbling for a while. The house smelt wonderful for those who like such smells. Laura was still nowhere to be seen. "I'll go and see," said Liz.

Laura was still fast asleep. Liz gave her a gentle push on her shoulder. "Fancy some breakfast with the rest of us, Laura?"

Laura stirred, opened her eyes, sat bolt upright and said "Oh God, am I late? Jesus. I can't be late. What will they do to me?"

"It's OK, Laura. It's OK. Liz here. No problem. Just some breakfast for the four of us—you, Tom, me and Gavin."

"Oh. Thank goodness for that. For a moment I thought I was back…well…you know, sort of…well…back…home…you know." Liz didn't comment. Whatever it was, it would keep.

It was a beautiful morning, so they sat around the table on the front terrace under the bougainvillaea, which spread out across the partly open roof, providing much-needed shade from the sun, especially in the summer. Even Liz, who had cooked hundreds of breakfasts, had to admit it was a great one. Strangely, the talk didn't turn once back to the conversation the evening before. In fact, there was very little talk. Everyone was too preoccupied relishing the smoked bacon and Lincolnshire sausages (both bought from the local *Overseas Markets* store, which was, in fact, a UK 'Iceland' outlet, now quite common in 'expat Spain'), fried tomatoes, eggs and the rest. When anyone did start to talk, it was more about the morning UK TV news, brought to them via their satellite dish on the solarium: two motorist deaths in a major pile-up on the M6; a student missing from university; continuing war and strife in the Middle East; more claims of child sex abuse among politicians and so on. To be frank, the news was much the same every day—unrelenting darkness—or so it seemed to Tom and Liz. However, over coffee, it was clearly time to continue the conversation from the evening before.

"So, suppose we're now back at Fairholme. You've spotted the bastards and are monitoring them through the bugs you've planted. They have a go-to bump us both off, fail—or succeed I suppose—and then scarper for it. What happens then?" Tom expected all this had been covered in the planning, but he wanted to know for sure.

Henderson topped up his coffee and said firmly, "They won't succeed, Tom. Part of the reason for us delaying things by driving back to your place is also to enable DCI Williams and at least two of our colleagues, to check-in to your friends B&B not far from you. Barnsley Charlie will have been alerted already by us, or whoever is in your larger room, that the hit is on, and he and our colleagues will be covering the front and back exits to your place."

"You mean Des and Anne?" Liz said with incredulity. "You're going to involve them? Why on earth involve them, for God's sake?"

"They're not being involved," said Laura. "They have simply taken a booking. No more; no less."

"So, have you both planned our route back to good old Blighty?" said Tom.

"Well, Barnsley Charlie said we should leave that up to you. You might know the best route since you drove your car down here," said Henderson.

"How the hell do you know that?" said Tom indignantly.

"We had to do our homework before we came on this trip, Tom. You'll understand that, I'm sure. We also know you have a Honda CR-V, first registered in the UK in 2000 and re-registered here last year. The number plate is 96…"

"All right, all right. You've made your point. But if you once even think of telling me the colour of my favourite boxers then I'll bop you one," Tom said, bringing a chuckle from Laura and Liz, who both knew full well—but for different reasons—that he'd come off much worse in a bout of 'fisticuffs' with Gavin.

"Anyway, given you know so much, you'll know the route we took then," Liz said, more than a little irritated by how much the Met did seem to know about them.

"Well, you crossed through the Channel Tunnel; drove south toward Rouen; then on to Bordeaux, crossing into Spain en route for Zaragoza and then down here to this great house." Swain reeled it off as if she had learnt it for an exam, hoping the reference to how lovely the house was might calm Liz's obvious temper a little. It didn't work.

"Bloody hell. Spot on. And I bet you know where we stayed overnight on the journey and what we had for breakfast," Liz said, now not so much irritated as practically boiling over with rage. This was an invasion of their privacy.

"No, we don't know that. We only know the route because your car was picked up a few times on CCTV during the journey, and we could piece it together from there," said Swain in a very matter-of-fact, neutral manner.

"So, when do we leave?" said Tom, trying to deflect things away from anything which might fuel Liz's obvious ill-temper.

They all looked at each other in turn, expecting someone to give an answer. Eventually, Gavin broke the silence.

"I suggest tonight. Laura and I can get our car back to the local police here in Cabo de Palos today, and they will sort it out with the car hire company—if one of you will bring us back here in your car. After that, it should be a matter of packing-up, putting our four bags in the boot, and setting off."

"We'll need to do our usual decommissioning of the house—you know, gas, electricity, water and stuff. And, we haven't booked anywhere to stay on the journey. We stopped three times on the way down here," Tom said, now getting more and more excited by the prospect of the journey, though trying to conceal it from Liz who looked anything but excited.

"Well, I'm the one who usually does such things, so maybe Laura and I can spend the rest of today making some bookings on my iPad? Providing, that is, that you two clear-up all the breakfast things," she said, pointing at Gavin and Tom in turn.

"So, are we OK to leave tonight then?" said Henderson.

Liz and Laura shrugged their shoulders and nodded their heads. Then Liz said, "Best to have a good meal before we head off, though, don't you think?" They all nodded. The plan was agreed.

During the day, Henderson and Tom drove to the small police station in Cabo de Palos and sorted out the hire car. Once Henderson had shown his ID, it was all plain sailing. Meanwhile, Laura and Liz set about making hotel bookings. They decided on just two stops this time and settled on Zaragoza and Tours.

Liz eventually found receipts for the hotels they had used on the trip down and they got two rooms at the first attempt at the one in Zaragoza. The second overnight in Tours would mean a long drive from Zaragoza, but Tom and Gavin had agreed to share the driving anyway. *This shouldn't be too bad for Gavin*, Liz said to herself, *and if Tom shows signs of stress, then Laura or I could take over.* Liz had already said she was happy to take a turn at the wheel too, unless it was in the dark. Since she had had her lens replacement, she had become much less confident with night driving.

Laura said she could use the Met credit card she had been given to book the hotels, but she decided this might be unwise especially if one or more of the bastards, or their cronies, might be tracking them.

"Not very likely, is it?" Liz asked nervously.

"No, Liz. But better not take any chances however minute they are." Liz nodded and agreed they would use Tom's and her joint account debit card.

As they stood in the kitchen making final preparations for the meal, and putting together some bacon sandwiches, fruit, and coffee for the early first part of the journey, Tom couldn't help but comment, "Bloody fine thing, eh? We pay for the hotels and everything else I wouldn't wonder if it's left to those two. Well, they can bloody well pay for some food and some diesel and I'll make sure of that. They'll be able to claim it all on expenses anyway."

"Keep your voice down, Tom," Liz said in a muffled voice herself. "They're protecting us, remember? And they have a plan to put an end to this whole horrible saga. When you consider that, it ain't much for us to pay for a couple of hotels, a tank or two of diesel, and ninety quid or so for Eurotunnel, is it?"

"OK. OK. Got your point. But, remember, you're the 'war baby' who is always counting the pennies so, as you put it, 'the pounds will look after themselves', right?" Tom knew he was right, and Liz knew he was too. But this was different. Their lives were at stake.

Just at that moment, Gavin's head appeared around the corner of the wall between the living room and the kitchen.

"Anything either of us over here can do to help?" he said, with a willing tone to his voice. "That bacon smells delicious."

"Er, well, no," said Liz, immediately wondering just how much of her conversation with Tom he had heard. "It's all done. Just about to dish up on the dining table over there."

They settled down to the casserole which had been slowly cooking for the last three hours. Everyone but Tom had wine. He was driving. As they ate, Tom couldn't resist asking Gavin and Laura about themselves. *Afterall*, he thought to himself, *we're putting our lives in their hands, and on top of that, we'll be spending the next three days closeted together.*

"I was expecting you to ask at some stage," said Gavin. "Why don't we share histories on the journey. Gonna be a long time in that car together."

Seemed a good plan.

Chapter Eight

14 September 2002

According to the AA Route Finder, and Tom's much less reliable memory, the journey to Zaragoza would be about six-and-a-half hours including at least one food, comfort and diesel stop. There would be more comfort stops than that, but probably fairly quick ones, so they had agreed to set off about 1 am the following morning. This way, they should arrive at the hotel about 8:00 or 8:30 am—depending on whether they met any hold-ups—which was the time they had told the hotel they would arrive. The hotel had been very understanding and agreed their rooms would be ready for that time. They had also agreed to extend their checkout time until 1 pm from the normal 12 noon, giving them four or so hours' sleep before the long, next stage of the journey to Tours. Liz was a truly remarkable negotiator.

They left the house just before 1 am. They passed *'Restaurante Mosqui'*—a favourite with Tom and Liz and only five minutes' walk from their place—and the 'Gran Torino' where they sometimes went for an evening drink. Then it was straight out of the village passed the *EuroSpar* and *Iceland* supermarkets and petrol station—where Tom had filled-up the evening before—and on to the link road to the motorway.

Naturally enough, it was very quiet on the roads from the house and out of the village. Perhaps the only night it might have been different would be Saturday as late-night revellers returned home. *Thankfully*, Tom thought, *this is Tuesday and the only things to avoid will be the odd cat looking for its good night out*. Cabo was generally a very quiet place; ideal for the retreat which Liz and Tom wanted their Spanish hideaway to be; and not too far, but far enough, from more bustling places like Cartegena, La Manga and Los Alcazares.

After about twenty minutes or so, and once on the AP7 Motorway, Tom set the cruise control to 120 kph and then decided it was time to learn something about DS Henderson and DC Swain.

"So, Gavin, how about telling us a little bit about yourself?"

"OK. Why not?" He said a little awkwardly.

"Well, I was born and raised in Bedford. Went to the Pilgrim Fathers School where I was destined not to shine academically, it seems…or at least that is what all the teachers kept telling me. I was much more into sports. Rugby and cricket, mainly. Played for the school first teams at both and went on to play in the Bedfordshire County Cricket League when I was about 17." At that point, Laura piped up from the back,

"Can you speak up a bit, Gavin? It's hard to hear you back here."

"OK. Is this any better?" he said, rather over-doing the deliberate diction and louder voice.

"Cheers," said Laura and Liz almost simultaneously.

"So where was I? Oh, yes, cricket and stuff. Well, after school I went to the local FE College to do business studies. An HNC and then HND. Anyway, I met a couple of guys on the HND course from the county police and after talking to them quite a lot, I decided to try to become a copper. I guess the rest is, as they say, history."

Liz leant forward, putting her head a little way between the two front seats. "You don't have a southern-type accent, Gavin, for someone born and raised in Bedford. In fact, it's a strange accent if I'm honest."

"Well, I guess that comes from Italian heritage. My grandfather was Italian. He came to Bedford to work in the brickyards, like many, many, before him and also with him. His daughter married a local chap called Richard Henderson—my old man—but maybe some element of my mother's accent has stuck with me. You're not the first to think I speak 'a bit funny' as they would say."

"So, who do you support in the Rugby World Cup, or the Football one for that matter?" said Tom, bringing a chuckle from Laura and Liz.

"England publicly, and Italy privately," Henderson said with a grin. They all laughed and then the car settled down into a quiet spell. Gavin and Laura did stuff on their mobiles. Liz worked on cryptic crosswords from a pocket-sized book she had also bought with her from the UK.

They'd been travelling for nearly three hours and, despite lots of chit-chat about life in Spain, the weather, the politics, the culture, and similar stuff, and a comfort stop, Liz was getting nervous about Tom continuing to drive without a break. She asked everyone if anyone needed the loo. They didn't, but Tom spotted the real reason for the question.

"If memory from our last journey this way serves me right, we should get to a pretty good *Vente del Aire* on this motorway in less than another hour. Its *Venta del Alben...* doodah...something or the other. I was planning we'd stop there to fill up with diesel and maybe get some warm *tapas*. And, of course, use the facilities. Does that sound OK, Liz?"

Liz had been scanning the map using the interior rear lights in the car.

"It's called Albentosa, and it does if you're OK driving. Remember, this will be the longest drive you've done for a really good while and certainly, since...well...er...you know." She'd switched off the roof lights so no one could see, but she screwed up her face in a painful gesture at the thought of what had happened a little over six months ago.

They all got out of the Honda as if being peeled from their seats. It wasn't an uncomfortable car. In fact, Liz and Laura would have easily gone to sleep in the back had it not been for Tom and Gavin chatting incessantly in the front—generally about football, cricket and rugby. Tom's memory about who won what in which years and sports used to be fairly good, but now he could barely remember who won the last world cup. He was becoming increasingly frustrated by it, but thankfully, the *Albentosa Vente* soon appeared just a kilometre away.

Tom filled up with diesel whilst the others headed straight to the *Venta* for the toilets and to order some hot food. The food Liz had prepared for the journey had been devoured long ago, and they all yearned for warming food. Over their *tapas* of *Albondigas* (small meatballs in rich tomato sauce—an absolute favourite of Tom), *patatas fritas* (truly wonderful large, chunky chips), bread and salad, Tom revisited the matter of 'personal histories'.

"Well, I think maybe you or Liz should spill the beans this time," said Gavin as he dipped the crusty bread into his second bowl of *Albondigas* in the rich tomato sauce only the Spanish seem to know how to make. "Seems only fair, don't you think?"

"Sure thing," Liz said, "In any case, it'll be easier here over this table than in the car where it's bloody hard to hear each other. I'll have a go." She settled into her seat, poured some more diet coke and began.

"I was born into a farming family in the northeast of England and raised on a small farm not far from Hexham with two brothers—one of them my twin—and a sister. Never thought of myself as a farmer but even so, I married one and had two boys by him. The marriage didn't work out and I moved out with the boys. Went on to teach shorthand-and-typing at a local school; eventually signed up for a university degree in business studies by evening study, and then got a lecturing job at the same university."

"Not quite rags-to-riches perhaps, but not far from it," said Laura, sipping her second, truly wonderful coffee with brandy, "But how the hell did you go from that to marrying Tom?"

"Well, it's quite a long story, if you have the time."

"We've got days," said Gavin with a rueful smile. "Go for it."

"OK."

Chapter Nine

Morning of 10 September 2002

Naz knocked on the door and was greeted with a stern come in'.

"Well?" said DCI Williams.

"I think you'll find that DC Swain and DS Henderson are nearly all ready to go, sir. They have the required documents."

"Great work, Naz. Get me a meeting with them as soon as you can. Oh, and by the way, get them relieved from any duties on any other cases they are working on for…say…the next three weeks."

"That will need your say-so, sir."

"Of course, of course! Just refer the supervising officer to me. If they need me to sign a chitty then that is fine. Just put it under my nose and I'll sign it."

For a moment, Naz wondered what else he might sign under such an arrangement, but the thought passed almost as soon as it had appeared. He immediately began to arrange the meeting with Swain and Henderson.

Two days later, Henderson and Swain were in Williams' office, with Naz to assist if necessary, with any of the travel details.

"OK. You have your documents, passports, etc and you know where you are going, yes?"

"Pretty much, sir," said Henderson, "But we aren't sure why we are going there and what we are doing once we are there."

"Christ almighty. What the hell do you do all day, Naz? Never mind, never mind. OK, here's the plan."

They sat around the desk and examined the layout of the local geography near to where Tom and Liz had their place in Cabo de Palos.

"Once you have your hire car sorted and have collected your 'hand jobs', you get as fast as possible to their place, and then convince them to travel with you back to the UK in their car. Easy. Yes?"

Swain and Henderson looked at each other, hoping the other had the right answer.

"Well, I get the first part, sir; but why would they want to travel 1,600 miles back to the UK with Swain and me?"

"Because DS Henderson, you and we are going to set a trap to catch those who want to kill Tom Cooper. It goes like this: we bug their house while you are travelling back there from Spain. Naz and I get ourselves as paying guests into the B&B near to their place for a stay during the early days after your arrival. When you arrive, you and Swain move into their largest room. It has a king-sized bed, so this shouldn't be a major problem, I think?" DCI Williams winked at Henderson. DC Swain flushed a little and hoped that the DCI hadn't seen. "You will both get alerts by SMS when we believe the assassin has booked into the other room in Tom and Liz's B&B. You text us. We block all exits and you nab the bastards."

"OK, sir," said Henderson, "but will Dr and Mrs Cooper be expecting us?"

"Of course not!" said Williams, clearly frustrated and exasperated by the question. "If they were expecting you, can you imagine how many signals they would give to everyone around whilst waiting for you to arrive? We've no idea if they are under surveillance at this moment, and if they are how it is being done. But bear in mind always, their demise is a major job being planned by some very big players. They are not messing about."

"Thank you, sir."

Henderson and Swain got up from the desk and left the briefing room. On their way out down the corridor, Henderson asked Swain, "What the hell does 'demise' mean?"

Three days later, after making sure all was well at work and at home, and finalising all the documentation, they set off for Spain.

Chapter Ten

14 September 2002

"Well, we were thrown together, as you might say, during a university trip to the States. There were about 25 of us—senior lecturers like me, principal lecturers like Tom, heads of department and so on—representing many of the university's academic fields. It turned out that a group of us—four or five—gravitated to one another and spent time together when we could. I thought Tom was OK; good to be with."

"Seems he had bigger ideas, eh Tom?" Tom looked vaguely embarrassed and threw himself with some gusto into his salad.

"Well, anyway, when we got back to the UK, Tom kept up the contact. We lived about sixty miles apart, so it was mainly by telephone unless we met on the campus. I kept thinking, *He needs someone younger than me*, and set about finding him a possible younger partner. In the end, when I suggested a younger woman, whom we both knew he might have liked to date, his reply was, 'So, isn't there any mileage in our relationship?' He wasn't referring to the 60 or so miles between where he and I lived. He suggested a New Year's Eve trip to Amsterdam and, the rest, as they say, is history. We got married the following August."

"Goodness, Tom, you don't mess around, do you?" Gavin said, with more than a hint of admiration.

"Some of us have it, others don't," Tom replied, as deadpan as he could manage, but with more than a twinkle in his eye and a wry smile across his face.

By now, it was time to get going again. Gavin offered to drive in order to give Tom a break, and he accepted gladly.

"You'll need to do some driving tomorrow too," Tom said, as they walked to the car. "And, Liz too for that matter. It's a really long leg even compared to this morning."

Gavin and Liz replied almost in unison, "No problem," and off they set.

They hadn't gone more than ten kilometres before Tom was asleep, leaning on Liz's shoulder in the back of the Honda. Liz followed him very soon afterwards. Gavin and Laura thought it not wise to talk. There would be plenty of time to contact the boss with a progress report once they were in the hotel in Zaragoza. So, a very quiet CR-V sailed along for the next two hours or so until they reached the outskirts of Zaragoza. Laura decided it was wise to wake-up the dreaming couple, so everyone could help with the final directions. It wasn't necessary as it happened. The satnav performed magnificently, and Gavin—just as heroically—never took a wrong turn through the early-morning rush hour traffic in what was a *very* busy and raucous city.

After checking in, everyone went to their rooms. Tom and Liz were now wide awake, having slept—or as Tom called it, 'cat-napped'—pretty much all the way from Albentosa to the edge of Zaragoza. They unpacked some things but said very little.

"This is so bloody strange, sweetheart. Here we are in Zaragoza again and *still* unable to explore the city. And this time with two coppers in tow. It all feels so odd."

"All I want is a cuddle for a while with my husband, followed by a warm, solid breakfast and some very good coffee."

"You have such a way with words," Tom replied with a cheeky smile.

Eventually, they made their way down to the breakfast room and gorged on the display of warm, self-service fare and delicious coffee on offer. They didn't see Gavin or Laura at all before they went back to their room.

They had checked in with the boss, showered and changed clothes and then had gone downstairs to have their sumptuous breakfast. Afterwards, they enquired of Tom and Liz with the very helpful young woman on the reception desk which was set at the end of one of the most magnificent, and huge entrance halls to a hotel they had ever seen. Massive marble pillars rose out of the marble floor; the doors to the lifts were a red and gold colour, almost impossible to describe accurately; the lighting came from five massive chandeliers— the same colour as the lift doors—with twenty lights on each. Gavin reckoned that had it not been for the lights, it would have been possible to have a football match in this vast space. "A bit tricky playing on this marble," Laura had said with a wry smile.

Having discovered that, as far as the receptionist knew, Dr and Mrs Cooper had retired to their room after breakfast and hadn't left the hotel since. Gavin and Laura did likewise. Like the Coopers, they were both knackered and with that warm sated feeling now starting to overwhelm them, sleep beckoned as an irresistible urge.

All their alarm clocks went off just after 12 noon—each of them knowing they were due to leave the hotel no later than 1pm. They all met in the grand hotel entrance, settled the bill and were gone. The trip to Tours had started.

Chapter Eleven

15, 16, and Very Early 17 September 2002

They all knew that the drive to Tours was the longest stretch they would do on the journey back to Fairholme. And they all knew each of them would probably need to do a stint at the wheel. Tom was first at the wheel and pretty soon they were out of the city and heading north.

They approached the Spanish-French border crossing at Irun much sooner than any of them expected; such was the pace at which Tom had driven this leg of the journey, and because they had had no major delays except the usual slow traffic around Pamplona. Irun was where Tom and Liz had crossed into Spain on their journey south, and whilst they had been surprised then that there was no passport control; it obviously now came as no surprise at all as they sailed through the border and on into France.

Not far into France, they stopped for a comfort break and afterwards, Liz took over at the wheel. Once back on the road, Liz suggested it was high time that Laura told them something about herself, or maybe Tom.

"OK. I'll do my bit," Laura said, somewhat sheepishly but wanting to get it over and done with.

"I was born in Bristol to Irish parents. My father worked on the docks and my mum stayed at home to look after us kids. There were seven of us, so as she used to say she had a full-time job—it was just that nobody called it that in those days."

"I'll say it was a full-time job," Liz interjected. "It was hard enough looking after two boys."

"Anyway, I left home when I was about 16 and worked in various jobs such as stacking shelves in the local supermarket until I went out with a young copper who encouraged me to think about joining the force. Never thought of me wearing a services uniform but I applied, got in, and the rest is pretty much a simple story of being promoted to where I am now."

"Not married then?" Liz asked.

"No, Liz. And no children either. I think being raised along with six brothers and sisters has probably put me off the idea for life."

"Just as well you met that young copper I would say, Laura," Tom said from the front of the car. "Otherwise you might still be stacking shelves instead of seeing the French countryside, hurtling along to execute a cunning plan to catch some filthy bastards." Laura didn't respond.

It seemed only fair that Tom should now tell everyone something about himself. Like any good teacher, he decided to increase the suspense and eagerness to hear by saying he would share his background after their next comfort stop. By the time they had had that, including some food, it was well past seven o'clock in the evening. Liz had taken her turn at the wheel in the daylight, which she had made clear was the only way she would take a turn. They were now over halfway to Tours, and Gavin took the wheel.

"OK, Tom. You can't put it off any longer," said Gavin.

"All right. But I don't know why you want Liz and me to share our background. You must have read it all before in your police files."

"Sure. But it's never the same as hearing it from the horse's mouth, if you'll pardon the expression."

"OK. Here goes."

"I was born about seven miles from Birmingham in the so-called Black Country. Legend has it that the name came from a comment by Queen Victoria as she observed the miles and miles of factories and terraced house chimneys belching black smoke; covering everything with soot, on a train journey north from London. Anyway, Dad came from a middle-class family of shopkeepers and Mum from a working-class family. In the end, Dad left the family business, and for the rest of his life did a number of semi and unskilled jobs. Mum worked as a shorthand typist. I went to university, did three degrees—the perpetual student you might say—and then went on to teach at university. The rest as they say—"

He was interrupted by a chorus of 'is history', followed by more laughter than this poor attempt at a joke deserved. Tom began to wonder if they were all suffering from 'cabin fever'.

"Anyway, it wasn't all as simple as that given the events which bring the four of us closeted together in this tin can. There were the events in Belfast and the shoelace, the paperclip, and the pencil, not to mention the A4 paper and, of course, the book inside that damned briefcase in Bonn." As he said the words, he felt what seemed like icy water run down his back. He shivered.

"Those must have been very dark days, Tom," said Gavin. Tom nodded but said no more.

After that, Liz and Laura settled down in the back of the car and began to doze. Tom certainly felt like doing the same, but there was an unspoken agreement that anyone in the passenger seat would stay awake and help the driver to do the same. Once again, Gavin and Tom began to talk football and cricket. In some ways, these chats—trying to recall great games or players—were good for Tom. They helped exercise his memory. However, despite it feeling as if he could remember more than he might have done a few weeks ago, he still became really frustrated—not to say angry—because his recall was still not what it had been. Sometimes, in more reflective moments, he began to realise what it must feel like for those in the early stages of dementia—those still able to realise that their memory was failing; sometimes, despite specific prompts to try and remember that name, that place, that time.

Gavin decided he was fresh enough to continue driving the final leg to Tours after their final short comfort break. Laura wasn't sure he should do that, but he was insistent, and Tom didn't argue. It looked as if they would arrive at the hotel sometime around midnight, which was maybe an hour or so later than Liz had suggested to the hotel when she made the booking. She decided to text them just to be sure of no problems when they arrived. The text came back in French, which for a while made her completely non-plussed—a result more of being very tired and travel-weary than of anything else. It read: *Le personnel de nuit sera de service et a été informé de votre arrivée tardive.*

"Eventually," she said, "the night porters have been told that we will be late. All OK, it seems."

They arrived as four very weary travellers, checked in, said a very brief 'Good night all' and collapsed into their beds.

The following morning revealed filthy weather. The rain was lashing the windows of the breakfast room when they eventually made it down there, and it was dull and very cloudy. The temperature had also fallen considerably overnight, so it was a case of donning those warmer clothes they had all packed. Over breakfast, Tom joked that it would probably be like this all the way to York. He had never seen himself as a prophet, but he was soon to realise just how prophetic he was on this occasion.

"Well, I sincerely hope the weather isn't like this," Gavin said with more than a hint of seriousness in his voice. "We've still got a lot of driving to do. So far, it's been fairly straight forward, and the weather has helped enormously." It was now just before 10 am and although they had hoped to have longer rests out of the car, and even walk around Tours and stretch their legs, they decided to head to Calais immediately.

"We might as well, as there's no point in walking around in this weather." Tom said a little ruefully.

The drive to Calais was, as Gavin had hinted, truly awful. Road spray from the hundreds of trucks on the road to the ferry ports made visibility very, very poor. No chance of driving at the maximum allowed speed, as they had been able to do for virtually the whole journey from Cabo de Palos to Tours. They had originally planned to get the 18:00 hours train through the Tunnel and it now seemed just as well they had set off almost two hours earlier than planned. The conditions meant that driving was much more tiring than it had been so far, as well. Tom decided to drive the whole leg to Calais.

"No offence, everyone, but if we are to have a prang, then I'd rather say it was me at the wheel. Our Spanish insurance does cover all of you to drive, as you know, but this is our motor, so I think it only fair I take the responsibility given the conditions." No one argued. In fact, they all silently gave a deep sigh of relief at Tom's decision.

They did arrive in time for the six o'clock train. The weather was still very much the same, as it had been when they left Tours, so it was quite a relief to be loaded onto the train and bring to an end the incessant pounding of the rain on the car which they had endured for the last six-and-a-half hours—over an hour more than the journey should have taken. Tom was very, very drained after such a drive and he would now have just forty minutes on the train to recuperate before the last leg of the journey. However, there was no chance that Liz, Laura or Gavin were going to let him near that steering wheel after what he had just done.

"No chance, Dr Tom Cooper," Liz said in her sternest and, 'don't even think about arguing with me' voice. Tom knew it was pointless even thinking about it. Gavin decided he would do the first leg and Laura the second one. Again, Tom didn't argue.

They came off the train and were very soon heading towards the M20 and M25, finally to go north to York on the M1, A1(M) and A64. Despite everyone hoping the train door would open to reveal a beautiful September evening, they saw the same grey sky and torrential rain they had just left in Calais. Their hearts sank, thinking about the five or so hours ahead of them, on some of the busiest trunk roads in the UK; battling yet again with all the HGVs and the continuous spray. A quick check on Tom's phone showed that low pressure was sat over northern France and southern England as far north as Sheffield. It had moved slowly northward during the day having originally been sat over the whole of western France and just the most southerly English counties.

"Just our luck," Gavin said in a fairly despondent tone. "If it keeps moving northwards, we *will* have this damned weather all the way home." Tom looked sheepish. No one answered.

The journey north was exactly as they had predicted. Slow, highly stressful on the driver but also on everyone else who all seemed to be driving the car too. Once Laura had finished her leg of the trip near Sheffield, Tom said he would do the final stretch as he knew the way really well having done it so many times over the years, especially through his regular trips to see his elderly and failing mum in the Midlands.

They arrived at Fairholme at 12.30 am. All very relieved to be in one piece and also all really fed up with being trapped solely in each other's company. Liz and Tom got Fairholme up and running again, and the heating blasting out as hard as it could. They showed Laura and Gavin to their room where, very conveniently, the king-sized bed was already split into two. "Must have had a premonition you'd be with us," she said looking at a very bleary-eyed Gavin. He didn't respond, and Liz knew it was time to leave them alone.

She and Tom sat in the living room, roasting their feet in front of the gas coal-effect fire; Liz with a huge glass of her favourite Verdejo white wine and Tom with an even larger Australian Shiraz. They didn't speak for what seemed to both like a very short time but was, in fact, many minutes. Tom broke the silence.

"Well, sweetheart. We're both exhausted now, but when I think of what lies ahead, I suspect this is nothing to how we will feel in a few days' time."

Liz nuzzled up to him. "I know you are right, but I can only think about now. Warm and safe in our beautiful home, protected by two coppers upstairs." She drained her wine and said, wearily, "Time for the sleep of all sleeps."

Chapter Twelve

15 and 16 September

"DCI Williams here. Poor line. Can you say that again? They're not WHAT? What the hell do you mean? Well go and find out where the hell they are. Call me once you have further news—and don't worry about what time that is. Use my mobile."

Henderson looked at Swain. "Well, you could probably hear that for yourself given how loud he was shouting. We've got some genuine detecting to do, and by the sound of it, we haven't got long to come up with an answer."

"Where do we start? I guess we ask the neighbours to begin with?"

Henderson headed up the street and Swain down it. Should they encounter anyone who didn't speak English, it was likely to be quite a short conversation. No one had thought to help them with some smatterings of Spanish—or French for that matter—for the journey back to the UK. Now, they needed it for a whole different set of reasons.

For some time, they both found no information from any neighbours about where Tom and Liz might be. It was past eleven o'clock in the evening and all anyone could say was that it would be unusual for 'the Coopers' to be out much beyond this time of night.

Eventually, having drawn a blank with the neighbours, they went down to the harbour and marina and looked in the bars, restaurants and cafés to see if they could spot them. They had never met Tom and Liz, but they had been given good photos of them and good descriptions by the DCI. They were looking for a middle-aged, white, man and woman. He was almost completely bald and of medium height. She had blond hair and smaller than he was. Given how many people they saw met this basic description, it was a good job they had the photographs.

The harbour and marina were still buzzing with people even at nearly midnight. Many of the bars and restaurants were still quite full. They took their time. They even had a drink in one bar. However, their care and attention to the task bore no fruit. It was time to call the DCI.

"Right. You two get yourselves rooms for the night. Get to the Cooper's place tomorrow morning and hope to God they have come back from wherever they are staying."

DCI Williams sounded annoyed, nervous, and curious. This wasn't like him at all, thought Henderson.

The following morning, they ate a traditional Spanish breakfast of freshly squeezed orange juice, coffee, and 'tostados con tomate' in the small hotel they had found the night before. The small baguette was clearly only just out of the oven and, when smeared with wonderful olive oil, topped by the crushed tomatoes and salt and pepper, was a true delight. They both had two coffees before booking a further night—just in case the Coopers weren't at home—and then headed up the hill to the Cooper's place. There was no sign of the car and no one at home. It was just after 11:00 am. Time to brief Barnsley Charlie.

"OK, Jack. I am starting to get a bad feeling about this. I want you to contact the local police and request they run a check to see if they can trace where that Honda is. You know the drill—accidents, stolen vehicles, and the rest. They will probably point you to the *Guardia Civil*, so in the meantime, I'm going to liaise with senior officers in the Guardia in that region; explain what we are doing and ask if they can help us in any way. We'll speak again in a couple of hours. If they turn up in the meantime, then text me, and we can revert to our original plan."

The local police officers were very curious about the requests which Swain and Henderson put before them. They asked them to wait whilst they contacted an interpreter, who

147

they regularly used with people who did not speak much Spanish, and because their own English was patchy too—good enough to deal with tourists in most situations—but, they worried, perhaps not with something as serious as this.

Once everyone was clear what was being said, the senior police officer explained why they were so confused and curious.

"You see, we assisted two officers, from the London Metropolitan Police Force a few days ago, who were also looking for Dr and Mrs Cooper. We helped them obtain a hire car which they returned to us on the 13th, three days ago. You will no doubt soon ask me about their passports and IDs. Well, they had IDs which looked exactly like yours, including their names—only the man's first name was Gavin and woman's was Laura."

Long before she had finished, Jack Henderson had turned pale and Ginny Swain felt sick.

"Do you know where they went or where they were planning to go," Henderson said, in the calmest voice he could muster.

"No. We only know they went to visit Dr and Mrs Cooper. And, in any event, how do we know you are genuine, and they are not?"

"You can call our senior officer at The Met, Detective Chief Inspector Charlie Williams, and he will confirm. Here is his number. But *please*, can I ask you *not* to refer to the other people and leave that to me to explain to him?"

The senior officer disappeared, taking Jack and Ginny's IDs with him, followed by the interpreter. He returned twenty minutes later and confirmed he was happy to accept their story. He returned their IDs and asked if there was anything further he could do to assist them. Henderson asked if he could help to get the Guardia Civil to try and trace the CR-V through various searches, as he had discussed with DCI Williams earlier. He also asked if he, or any of his officers, could provide a full description of the imposters or whether, perhaps, the car hire company might have copies of their IDs. The senior officer explained that the car hire company would not have taken any copies given the couple were being introduced to them by the police.

"Ah, yes, I see," Jack said. "Very clever of them. But I presume you have copies of their IDs?"

There was a noticeable fall in temperature in the room at this point.

"I am afraid; we have such few officers here to cover all the things we must do. The officer here that day was very, very busy with many requests. He didn't make copies."

Swain and Henderson thanked everyone for their help and their honesty and were reassured to know that the interpreter—a woman born in England but raised from the age of five in Spain by bilingual parents—who was clearly superb at her job, had agreed to help them further if they needed it. The senior officer said her bill would be covered by the local police. *A way of saying sorry about not having copies of the IDs*, Henderson thought to himself.

Nevertheless, and once outside the police station, Henderson swore repeatedly about the fact the local copper hadn't made copies of the IDs. He was really, really angry, and for a moment, Ginny thought he was going to slam his fist into a nearby wall out of sheer frustration.

"But we've all been there," she said, trying to pour water on the flame and putting a consoling arm around his shoulders. "Are you so senior now you don't remember being the only front desk sergeant with more cons to be processed and more paperwork to complete in an eight-hour shift than could be done by any two normal human beings in 24 hours?"

"All right, all right! Time to call Williams. See what he says."

"We need more information before we can make any move, Jack. Most of all, we need those descriptions of the kidnappers. Any news on the Honda will be great, but if we can trace the kidnappers through our databases and those at Interpol, we'll know more about what we are dealing with here."

"But do you have an inkling?"

"Yes. But too early to share over an open line. Go and enjoy yourselves by the sea. Not to be done for some time today, I suspect. Once they send those descriptions through to me, as they agreed, I'll call you…so, no getting thoroughly ratted on cheap plonk or G&Ts."

As they walked back to the harbour and marina to follow their orders to 'enjoy themselves by the sea', Ginny said, "I don't think I've been impersonated before. Makes you feel quite important doesn't it?"

Jack was staring ahead and only half heard what she said.

"Important? Oh, sure, yeah. But say that to the families of those two poor buggers when you're at their funerals."

Ginny said nothing for a good time that afternoon, and neither did Jack. Then, his mobile rang.

Chapter Thirteen

17 September, Fairholme

By the time Tom and Liz emerged from their 'pit'—as several of Tom's friends routinely referred to 'bed'—Gavin and Laura were already in the middle of making coffee and searching for bread in the freezer to make toast. They all worked out how to make their breakfasts without saying very much at all to each other. After all, they had talked, chatted, had several more serious conversations, shared their histories and just travelled, closeted together in one car, for three days. What more could there be to say to each other? Eventually, once everyone was settled with toast or cereal, or just freshly brewed coffee as in Tom's case, Gavin broke the virtual silence.

"Seems like the storm has passed," he said, pointing through the breakfast room window towards the blue and fluffy-white, patchy cloud sky. They all looked and nodded a little like robots.

"I've had a call from the boss and there is a slight change of plan." Tom and Liz immediately awoke as if from a dream and leant forward across the table expectant of more information.

"The basic plan hasn't changed. We are hoping you will open up your second bedroom to new visitors and they will be checked to decide if they are 'the bastards'. However, Laura and I will check into your friend's B&B along this road rather than staying here. This way, we can be much better placed to surprise 'the bastards' once they have checked into Fairholme. You will still be fully covered including, remember, your 'minder' out there." Gavin pointed vaguely outside.

There was a long silence.

Gavin looked at Laura and she at him. Liz stared down at her plate and cradled her coffee.

Tom broke the silence. "But that note on our doormat said our minder wouldn't be any use. That is why the plan was for you to be staying here."

"Yes, it did, Tom. But that was without them knowing we will also be just a moment away, *and* we'll have a head start on them because we will know in advance who they are."

"So, when do *we* get to know that the bastards have landed?" Tom said, in a very calm, almost other-worldly, and distant, voice.

"You will know as soon as we do, Tom," Gavin replied, almost instantly. "And we will get you out of the way," he added quickly.

"We will be going out now, to explore York, and wait for any messages about your bookings. All you need to do is to take all those calls, record as much information from each of them as possible, and then let me know by text the crucial information you have about them—names, addresses, telephone numbers, date of arrival, length of stay, car reg. if they have one, and so on. The more the better, but without sounding too prying—which I am sure you never are, Liz— which could give the game away. We will be in touch with you by text should we suspect anything. Our colleagues will be here like a flash and we won't be far behind."

Tom and Liz were still not really fully awake but they both nodded at which Gavin and Laura left the breakfast room and went on their tour of York.

Gavin and Laura walked towards the river and turned left towards the city centre. They hadn't gone far when the call that Gavin was expecting came through. He sat down on a nearby riverside bench to take it and handed the mobile to Laura.

"DB here. Safe to talk?"

"Yes."

"Right. Listen very carefully. There will be a silver BMW parked, engine running, in the road opposite the one of your B&B across the main street. It will be there from 22:00 to 22:10 exactly. Do your work by then and the car and driver are there for you. If not, you are on your own."

The phone clicked off.

Chapter Fourteen

Morning of 16 September

"Yes, sir?"

"OK. I'll give you the bare bones of what we now know, so you better take notes." Williams' voice was strong and clear, back to what it was normally.

"The two imposters are known to Interpol. The one posing as you, DC Swain, is thought to be Marianne von Strauss, daughter of Monika von Straus who was implicated in the briefcase incident in Bonn with Tom Cooper. Your impersonator, Jack, is Michael van Voet. He is the half-brother of the guy who Tom Cooper met in Bonn. We believe, they both report to Declan Brophy, at least for this job. And we also believe that von Strauss is the paymaster's preferred 'hitman'…so to speak."

"Bloody hell," Jack said.

"It gets worse," Williams said, "so listen up."

"I have reasons to believe the four may be on their way to York or are there already. The Honda was spotted going through the border between France and Spain at Irun. It was also recorded on the Channel Tunnel." He took an audible deep breath.

"You now need to get back to the UK as fast as possible and head straight for York. Don't worry about flight costs, taxis, train fares or whatever. It will be covered. Just get to York rail station as fast as you can. Keep me updated, and I will meet you there. Understood?"

"Yes, sir, but what if we can't get a flight for a day or two from this part of Spain?"

"You're not listening to me, Jack? Hear me now. Get the first available flight from Spain to London or Manchester or Newcastle or Leeds Bradford, or even Bristol or Bournemouth, or anywhere else for that matter. If that happens to be from Madrid or somewhere else, then make sure you get it. Am I making myself clear now, Jack?"

"Yes, sir."

Once in the picture, Ginny began to search for potential flights using her iPad. It wasn't promising.

"They're all fully booked, Jack," she said, after about 40 minutes of silence between them.

"Keep trying, Gin. Remember any outward airport and any home airport. The only criterion is that we have time to catch the bloody plane. After that, we use whatever means necessary to get to York as fast as is humanly possible." Jack sounded as frazzled as Ginny felt. After another 30 minutes and several more cups of coffee in the café where they had been sitting all morning and using their wi-fi, Ginny exclaimed,

"GOT ONE!!"

"It's a cancellation. Two seats. Alicante to Leeds-Bradford. Leaves in two hours. Can we get there in time, Jack?"

"Book it. We'll get there." Jack had absolutely no idea whether it could be done but he would give it his very best.

They sped out of Cabo as if being followed by the devil himself. Jack had decided that if stopped by any coppers, they would get them to call DCI Williams to explain it was life or death. Ginny tried to use Google Translate to get those words in Spanish using Bluetooth on her phone.

"If we need it, the phrase is: *Soy un oficial de policía del Reino Unido. Tengo que llegar al Reino Unido lo más rápido posible. Esta es una cuestión de vida o muerte.*"

Ginny's Spanish pronunciation was far from perfect. In fact, it was awful. But Jack knew this mattered not one jot. If they were pulled over, it would probably do the trick, especially coupled with their IDs and DCI Williams' telephone number for their bona fides.

"Great stuff, Ginny," he shouted, above the raucous engine noise of a 2001 Ford Ka being pushed to its limits. As it happened, Jack didn't need to experience the trauma of hearing Ginny attempt the phrase in Spanish again. In fact, plenty of cars raced past them making it look as if Jack was peddling the Ka even though he was doing well over the 120 kph speed limit.

They raced into Alicante-Elche Airport, parked in the short-stay car park and legged it up the ramp into departures. For once, Ginny began to thank the trainers who had put them through their paces as new recruits all those years ago and the regular fitness tests they were now required to undertake. She swore at them then. She didn't now.

Chapter Fifteen

Fairholme, Evening of 17 September

Tom and Liz had had almost all day to recover from the journey; for once alone together for a good few hours.

Liz had taken calls for bookings and, as required, had taken as many details as she could without appearing 'to pry' as Gavin had put it that morning. She had texted Gavin with that information as soon as she had the chance. He hadn't responded yet, but then she really hadn't expected he would. There would be checking to do, and that takes time.

As the evening began to close in, Tom and Liz's thoughts turned to an evening meal. They started to prepare one of their favourites: chicken with mushrooms, sun-dried tomatoes in olive oil, tarragon seasoning, bound together by white wine and cream sauce.

They prepared enough for Gavin and Laura and, if they didn't return for it or want it, it could be frozen as they had often done in the past. As it happened, they appeared at the front door with precision timing.

They all sat down to the meal, with Tom and Liz eager to learn what the two visitors had made of their city. As a kind of celebration for making it this far, Tom opened a bottle of Cava and poured everyone a glass.

"To safe passage and safe life," he toasted. They all sampled the Cava with noises of sheer delight at its fragrance and lightness. The fact that neither Gavin nor Laura repeated the toast completely bypassed Tom and Liz.

As Tom went to get wine, port and brandy from the dining room to follow up after the dessert and Liz went back to the kitchen to complete the dessert, Gavin slipped a small pill into each of their Cava glasses.

They weren't long into the dessert before Tom and Liz began to feel both very drunk and also very tired. Within a few minutes, and before they knew what was happening, they were both asleep, heads slumped onto the table. At this point, and as planned, Gavin and Laura went upstairs to change clothes and collect their few things. Gavin came back downstairs first and went into the breakfast room to check on Tom and Liz.

Laura followed him a few minutes later, but as she reached the final step of the stairway, there was a knock on the front door. She reached for her gun. As she did so, the front door burst open and Jack Henderson came through it with his handgun at the ready. He let off two shots. One hit the balustrade next to where Laura was standing. The other hit the middle of her chest, piercing her aorta.

As she stumbled forward onto the hallway floor, she fired straight at Jack. The first bullet hit him in the heart and the second, as she fell to the ground, in the groin.

Gavin, hearing the shots, locked the breakfast room door and jammed it with one of the dining room style chairs from around the breakfast room table. He moved to the back door which led from the kitchen out into the courtyard. At that moment he heard shouting from the hallway and people battering at the breakfast room door.

He turned and fired the final two assassins' bullets at Tom and Liz, still slumped over the breakfast room table…two for each of them. He didn't wait to see if they hit their mark; there was no time for that. He moved out into the courtyard and climbed silently onto the top of its seven-foot wall using the table at the far end—a favourite place for Liz and Tom to enjoy a glass of wine at the end of long working days, especially during the summer.

Dressed all in black and, in the darkness of the alley, he was virtually impossible to see—unless you knew he was there. He laid motionless and watched as two people silhouetted by the street lights behind them moved down the alley towards the courtyard gate. He re-loaded his gun.

Two shots fired. Two bodies lying crumpled on the cobbled alleyway floor.

Gavin slid down the courtyard wall and into the alley. He walked, very nonchalantly in the circumstances, away from the fallen bodies through another alleyway which led onto the street which ran parallel to that on which Fairholme stood. He took some deep breaths, turned left and walked the sixty-or-so metres to the main road which he crossed. Once on the other side, he turned left again and then right into the street where the silver BMW would be waiting. It was.

He opened the kerbside rear door and slid quietly, perhaps even serenely, into the rear seat. The car moved off, turned left onto the main road and into the city.

Chapter Sixteen

Two Days Later

DCI Williams paced repeatedly up and down.

There was a notice blue-tacked to the door of the small hospital ward. It read: 'NO VISITORS of any size, shape, colour, gender, sex, sexual orientation, or anything else. ONLY KNOWN DOCTORS AND KNOWN NURSES TREATING THESE PATIENTS.

Inside the ward sat a young WPC and outside a PC. As Williams was fond of recounting, "They both looked to be about 14, but I guessed they knew their job." Whether they did or didn't, they were both armed and with clear instructions to shoot any intruders other than the known doctors and nurses looking after Liz and Tom.

Tom and Liz had both recovered from the sleeping drug, but they were now in the early stages of recovering from the surgery they had both needed to remove the bullets fired by van Voet, and repair the damage they had caused. Liz had come off worst. One of the bullets had grazed the back of her skull. The other had entered her neck just above the collar bone. By the time she got into surgery, she had lost a great deal of blood and all her vital signs were right on the edge. One of the bullets fired at Tom had hit his upper arm, and the other was lodged just behind his right ear. He was not in good shape either by the time the surgeons got to him.

Neither had yet fully recovered consciousness. The process of recovering from the anaesthetic was hampered by the very powerful sleeping pills administered by van Voet. The DCI left the ward with instructions to the two PCs to call him as soon as the patients regained consciousness.

He got the call from the ward senior nurse about 6 pm the following evening. She had cleared it with the surgeons that the patients were probably now strong enough for a short—she emphasised the word short several times—visit from the DCI.

"Well, well, well, Dr and Mrs Cooper. So very good to see you looking this well after all this excitement."

"That's what you call it, eh?" croaked Liz.

"Not at all. I am very, very sorry. I was so flippant. Just trying to break the ice, you might say." The DCI looked down at his shoes. "I am here to try and explain to you what went on at Fairholme and before that too if I can."

Liz looked across at Tom who simply nodded.

"Well, it goes something like this..." The DCI paused and cleared his throat, pulled up a chair and sat in the corner of the room, facing them both.

"The idea that we might have a mole in the camp only occurred to me once it became clear that you had set off to the UK well ahead of our ability to come to you in Cabo de Palos but to make the same journey. That mole was DC Naz Ali. The reason he betrayed our plans to Michael van Voet—half-brother of the van Voet you met in Bonn, Tom—and to Declan Brophy doesn't really matter now, I suppose, but..."

"It matters to both of us I think, DCI Williams. What he did almost cost both of us our lives, so I think we have a right to know," Liz said with more than a hint of indignation.

"Yes, well, it seems he was more than a bit disgruntled at how he felt The Met had treated him—still only a DC after six years in CID, and having seen 'lesser coppers' as he saw them, promoted above him. It may seem an extreme way of signalling how pissed-off he was, but the opportunity came his way. Michael van Voet ran into DC Ali at a cricket match. They chatted, shared personal histories—in van Voet's case all a complete fabrication—and Ali chose to share his complete disgust with The Met and how he had been treated," Williams paused just long enough for Tom to interject,

"And I bet van Voet told him he was born in Bedford; was much more into sports than his studies—rugby and cricket mainly. Played for the school first teams at both and went on to play in the Bedfordshire County Cricket League."

"How on earth did you know all that?" Williams said, with complete incredulity.

"Because that's the bullshit he fed to us on the journey back to the UK, that's why," said Tom, full of spite and anger.

"Well, you have to remember, Tom, that van Voet inherited more than a little of his half-brother's acting skills. In fact, in his dirty underworld, there are those who are good, those who are very good, those who are amazing…and then there is Michael van Voet."

"You can say that again. They befriended us. We laughed and sometimes nearly cried together. We learned to respect each other. Can you believe that? They were so convincing that we learned to respect them. For three days, they kept-up this amazing charade. And why? All, in the end, to blow our brains out so as to settle someone else's score." Tom reached across to Liz in the other bed and felt for her hand dangling down the side of the bed. He squeezed it and looked at her, tears welling up in his eyes. "And they nearly succeeded, didn't they, DCI Williams?"

"Yes, but maybe that is enough for today. I was told this must be only a short visit."

"You're not going anywhere until we hear the full story," Liz said in that 'and no use arguing with me' tone of voice at which she excelled.

"OK, but if the senior nurse comes in, even you will have to accept what she says, as will I."

"So, where were we? Oh yes, they did nearly succeed. 'They', of course, being not just van Voet, but also his sidekick for this work. Namely, Marianne von Strauss." Williams knew the name would bring an immediate reaction at least from Tom if not from both of them.

"von Strauss!" Tom exclaimed, trying to sit upright.

"Don't do that, sweetheart. You have to lie as still as possible, remember?" Tom sank back into the pillow, but his eyes were still staring like those of the proverbial rabbit caught in the proverbial headlights. Williams got up from the chair and massaged his back whilst walking to and fro across the room in front of them.

"Yes, Tom, the daughter of your former partner in Bremen, Monika von Strauss. Monika never married, but had Marianne through one or another liaison she had in the early eighties. Marianne went to university in Gottingen where her mother had studied. During her studies of Italian, she went to work for her 'year out' in Milan. There she met the son of a certain Signore Luciano Copa and through him, Luciano himself. The father was connected to the mafia and the IRA through bankrolling certain—what shall I call them—'jobs'.

"But Monika would never allow her daughter to get caught up in such things, DCI Williams. She simply wouldn't allow it," Tom spoke clearly and passionately. "And in any event, Laura—as she called herself—looked nothing like Monika. There would have been some resemblance, surely?"

"I know you do not have any children of your own, Tom, but you work alongside enough twenty-somethings to know, I am sure that by that stage, the power of the parents to influence their decisions, values, ideologies, and so on is generally almost zero." Tom realised that what he said was true. This time it was Liz reaching out to squeeze *his* hand. "And, as to resembling her mother, Marianne is a true master of disguise. I bet even if her mother had been in the car with you, she wouldn't have recognised her."

"Anyway, back to where we were. She had a fling with Luciano's son, Milano, but it didn't last. After a few more dalliances, she moved to the States and by chance met our old friends the van Voets. All we really know from there on is that she is suspected of being involved in several 'jobs' funded by Luciano Copa. At university, she had become a crack pistol shooter and worked on make up with the university theatre group for at least two years. Enthused by the right-wing ideology of Luciano and Milano, working for them was a perfect fit. It was a highly lucrative dirty business too." Tom was deflated, but Liz wanted to know a little more.

"So, how come you know all this stuff about Marianne and what she gets up to?"

"Some of it is on file at Interpol but a lot of the more recent stuff has come through the ex-copper who was successfully planted as a driver and head of security for Signore Luciano Copa. He has also provided us with a clear link between Declan Brophy and the Copa family and that is why we believe he was the brains behind the plan which so nearly succeeded." Williams sat down again, now constantly looking at the door to this small ward, waiting for the senior nurse to come bursting through it at any moment. A short visit this was not.

"Ali had the full outline of our plan early on 10 September. Brophy, van Voet and von Strauss knew they would have to move quickly to get to you before we did. As soon as Brophy got a summary of *our* plan from Ali that day, he put the wheels in motion. Gavin and Laura—as you came to know them, but really Michael and Marianne—were already on standby (we think in London) and caught the first available flight out of Gatwick to Murcia San Javier. From there, as you will know much better than me, it was a short hop to Cabo de Palos. You know the rest only too well I think." Williams started to massage his lower back again and decided to get up and have another walk around the ward.

"The one part which we know nothing about, as yet, DCI Williams, is what happened at Fairholme after we had been drugged," said Liz in a pretty matter of fact sort of way. Tom was staring out of the window, still reeling from the news about Marianne von Strauss.

"Well, it isn't pretty." Despite needing more time on his feet, the DCI decided to sit down for this.

"Jack Henderson was killed just inside your hallway by shots from Marianne, but not before he had fired two shots of his own, which eventually killed her. Michael van Voet skipped out of your back door but before he left, and as a parting gift, shot at both of you twice. Thankfully, and as we now know, none of the shots hit their intended mark that is, your heads." Williams took a good gulp of water from the bottle he had with him and continued.

"van Voet shot two of our officers as he left the rear of your premises. They were DC Ginny Swain and DC Naz Ali. Both were fatally injured. Michael van Voet escaped somehow and to somewhere, and we are still looking for him." Williams knew this would unsettle both Tom and Liz and he had hoped not to have to share it with them this evening, but the Senior Nurse had not appeared to give him his legitimate exit.

"Oh...my...God. Oh, for Christ's sake," Liz said as loudly as the dressings around her upper body would allow. "Four people killed trying to either kill us or protect us. This is crazy. This is absolute madness. What the hell do we know that could be so dangerous to these people?"

DCI Williams took a final, and very large gulp from his bottle of water, and took a deep breath.

"The point is, Liz, they don't know what you know, or don't know, but are clearly unwilling to take *any* chances."

Unseen by DCI Williams, the ward senior nurse had very quietly entered the small ward and stood by the door next to the WPC as he delivered this final statement.

"So, you call *this* a short visit, and you think *that* is the kind of motivational speech to aid the recovery of two seriously injured people, DCI Williams?" The sarcasm was lost on no one in the room.

The reality of what the DCI had said just a moment ago was not lost on Tom and Liz as they went to sleep that night.

THE END

Several characters in this story are based upon real people. Names and some other aspects have been changed to protect their privacy.